Just One More Time

The Sterling Family
Book 6

NEW YORK TIMES BESTSELLING AUTHOR
Carly Phillips

Copyright © Karen Drogin 2025
Published by CP Publishing
Print Edition

Cover Photo: Wander Aguiar
Cover Design: Maria @steamydesigns
Editing: Rumi Khan and Claire Milto: BB Virtual Assistant for Authors

* * *

All rights reserved. No part of this book may be reproduced in any form by any means without the prior written consent of the Publisher, excepting brief quotes used in reviews.

This book is a work of fiction. Names, characters, places, and incidents either are products of the author's imagination or are used fictitiously. Any resemblance to actual events or locales or persons, living or dead, is entirely coincidental.

No part of this book may be used to create, feed, or refine artificial intelligence models, for any purpose, without written permission from the author.

This title claims exemption of the European Accessibility Act because the publisher qualifies as a micro-enterprise.

JUST ONE MORE TIME

One night. One heartbreak. One man she could never forget.

Years ago, Brooke Snyder gave her heart—and her innocence—to Aiden Sterling, her best friend's older brother. For one perfect night, he was hers. Then he walked away without looking back.

Heartbroken, she focused on her career, and tried to move on, while he was half a world away. But no man ever measured up to Aiden, and the one time she tried, ended in disaster.

Now, he's back to help his ailing father, and avoiding him isn't an option—not when they're forced to work together and *definitely* not when she's sleeping in the bedroom next to his.

The past crackles between them, charged with everything they never said and everything they still feel. Every look dares her to remember. Every touch reminds her exactly what she spent years trying to forget.

Giving him her body is easy. But how can she protect her heart... when the man who broke it is the only one who can put it back together?

Chapter One

BROOKLYN SNYDER ASSUMED the downward dog pose, her hands on the front of the mat, ass in the air. She stretched her feet out behind her, and blew out a long breath that sounded more like a pained sigh.

"Are you okay?" her friend, Amy, asked in between yoga stretches.

"Why wouldn't I be?" Brooklyn played dumb, stalling the inevitable conversation about her ex as long as possible.

From her own upside-down pose, Amy frowned. "We *are* going to discuss this after class."

Brooke had known Amy Jenkins since middle school where they'd sat together at lunch and had become inseparable ever since. If Amy said they were going to talk, she wouldn't be deterred, but Brooklyn was grateful for the end-of-class reprieve anyway.

Listening to the instructor, they stretched, then lay on their backs for Savasana, the resting pose. Was it bad that this was her favorite part of yoga? she mused.

Once the instructor released them, they rolled their mats, put other accessories away in the back, and walked out of the room together.

"Brooke, do you want to get a shake?" Amy pointed to the small café inside the gym with a few tables and a counter where the person working behind it made the most delicious chocolate and peanut butter protein shakes.

"Definitely." Her stomach rumbled in agreement.

They waited for the icy drinks to be created and luckily found a table where they could sit and talk. Or should she say *unluckily*, as Brooke didn't want to discuss anything related to Aiden Sterling, and that was definitely where this conversation was headed.

"Okay, so are you prepared to see Aiden at work next week?"

It was just like Amy to get right to the point, Brooke thought and groaned. "Couldn't you wait for me to at least enjoy my first sip before you started grilling me?"

"I'm not grilling you, I'm asking as a concerned friend. It's one thing to see Aiden on his occasional trips home, another to know he's back for a prolonged time, and yet *another* to have to work with him." Amy gave her a pointed stare.

Stalling, Brooke took a long pull from the straw and allowed herself to enjoy the chocolatey sweetness before meeting her friend's gaze. "With a little luck, we'll be working in the same office but not together."

During college, Brooke had interned for Sterling

Investments, and she'd been employed by them ever since. Yes, she'd known the family for years. When she was fourteen, the Sterling patriarch, Alex, had bought the estate where Brooke and her mother lived in the gatehouse. Alex had five children, and Brooke became close with each. Her mother remained the housekeeper and Brooke grew up with the family. Fallon, the only girl, was Brooke's other best friend and Brooke's mom was now dating Alex Sterling.

Brooke had earned her Chief Operating Officer position at the firm by working hard and dedicating long hours to proving herself. It helped that Aiden, who'd broken her heart, had been gone for five long years, and only returned for big events and when he could take time from his roving journalist job.

"Okay, but you still have to face him and talk to him. Or are you going to continue keeping him at arm's length?"

Brooke's heart skipped a beat at her friend's question. "Keeping Aiden at arm's length is for my sanity. I'm afraid if I get close to him, I'll slap him for all the pain he put me through."

"And he'd deserve it."

Brooke nodded. She'd given him her virginity and her heart, and he'd tossed her away the next day in favor of his career. He hadn't even allowed them the chance to make a long-distance relationship work.

He'd never taken her feelings and her needs into consideration. What she wanted hadn't mattered.

But that was in the past, even if the anger she felt was current and real. "I can handle seeing him," she said. "I've already done it at family get-togethers. I'll be fine." She wrapped her hands around the icy drink, the condensation seeping into her skin.

"And are you still keeping what happened from the family? You still won't tell Fallon?"

She shook her head. "Nobody knows. I don't want Fallon to feel like she has to take sides." Which was why she'd never told anyone but Amy what had happened with Aiden. Oh, they knew something had changed. Especially Brooke's mom. It was obvious she and Aiden were no longer close, but Brooke never spoke of why.

Holding her pain inside hadn't been easy but she'd done it once before, when her dad died, keeping things in so her mother wouldn't worry about Brooke while she dealt with her own grief. Continuing to pretend things with Aiden were fine but distant should be easy. She'd been doing it long enough.

She and Amy finished their drinks. Together, they walked out, parting ways at Brooke's PT Cruiser and Amy's SUV parked side by side.

"See you Wednesday night?" Amy asked. They met two times a week for yoga, Sunday mornings and

Wednesday evenings.

"I'll be there," Brooke said with a smile. She headed home to the gatehouse she still shared with her mother, not wanting Lizzie to be alone.

Aiden would be at work this coming Monday morning, and there wasn't a damn thing she could do about it.

Chapter Two

AIDEN WALKED INTO his father's home office, Alex Sterling's favorite room in the house. Times had changed and he no longer used the room for work. After his latest heart attack and surgery, he'd been instructed to cut back and relax more. He'd spent too much time ignoring doctor's orders and now, things were serious. Alex was forced to listen.

Jared, the only Sterling sibling who worked for the family business, had stepped up and taken over. But with Jared's baby due soon, Aiden would be helping out while his brother took temporary leave.

It had been a long time since Aiden considered working behind a desk. Once he'd made up his mind to follow his dreams, he'd happily ditched the idea of being indoors all day in favor of travel and news. But that was before. Before his family needed him. And before Aided decided it was time to step back from the reporting he loved.

"Aiden!" Alex rose to his feet, meeting Aiden halfway into the room and pulling him into a tight hug. "I'm so glad you're home."

He squeezed his dad tight. "Me too." No need to

think of the whys. Right now, Aiden was glad to be here.

"Come, sit. Lizzie left us iced tea and homemade cookies. She says they're chocolate but I know damn well they're carob. What the hell is carob?" he muttered, complaining about his new diet.

Lizzie, his housekeeper and current... could you call her his girlfriend at their age? Aiden held back a chuckle, just pleased his father was happy again after being a widower for so long.

"It's fine, Dad. Let's have some cookies while we talk. I'm sure they're good."

They settled into the two large, leather Queen Anne chairs in the room, the food on a tray sitting on the leather ottoman in front of them.

Aiden picked up a glass and took a drink of Lizzie's infamous iced tea and it was as delicious as he remembered. "Tell me, Dad. Are you really okay?" His father looked thinner, which was good for his health, and his coloring had returned. On their FaceTime calls post-surgery, Alex had been pale. "You look good."

His father nodded, rubbing a hand over the stubble on his face. "With my kids and Lizzie keeping me on the straight and narrow, yes. I'm fine. I'd rather hear about you."

Aiden's shoulder muscles tensed. He didn't want to discuss his last assignment, but he could reassure his father in other ways. "I have an article coming out in a few weeks and that will be my last one. I'm here to help Jared for as long as he needs me."

"And after that?" his father asked him.

"Then, I have decisions to make," Aiden admitted.

His dad raised his eyebrows. "What kind of decisions?"

Aiden shifted in his seat. "I'm done traveling."

Alex pinned him with a serious stare. "You gave up a lot here to report from abroad. Why the change?"

Rubbing the back of his neck, Aiden considered how to reply. He didn't want his father worrying, so he'd keep quiet about the danger in his last assignment. Danger that had followed him home. But there were other things about traveling he'd come to realize and those were truths he could share with his dad.

Aiden leaned on the arm of his chair, sliding his legs to the side in order to face his father. "Lately, I've done a lot of thinking about why I left in the first place."

"Well, you'd double-majored in business and journalism, so the job itself wasn't a shock. The travel aspect was."

Aiden nodded. He hadn't just shocked his family, he recalled, his mind drifting to Brooke, the girl he'd both hurt and let get away. He pushed thoughts of her aside because once he started working at Sterling

Investments, he'd see her every day and have to face that part of his past. Right now, there was something else he needed to come to terms with.

"The journalism part called to me. The travel, too, but for different reasons." He pressed his palms against his eyes. "It's about Mom," he said.

"Your mother?" His father sounded surprised. "What about her?"

Aiden let out a rough breath. "The night she was… killed," he said over a lump in his throat. "I was at camp. I don't think I ever got over the guilt of that. Of being away when she needed me. Of not being able to stop it."

Alex stared at him through now glassy eyes. He'd adored his wife, Gloria, and when a disgruntled client turned to drugs and killed her, his father had been destroyed. So had Aiden and his siblings.

"Son," he said in a broken voice. "You were twelve years old. If you'd been there and gone downstairs, I'd have lost you too, and I know I couldn't have coped with that."

Aiden managed a nod. "The adult me knows that, but the kid? I suppressed the feelings." Everyone was having a hard time getting over the trauma, and he'd never wanted to add to their pain, so he'd kept his own hidden.

"Taking the traveling journalism job was an escape.

I thought I'd be able to leave the memories and guilt behind. Instead, I realized it followed me wherever I went."

His father shook his head. "I wish I'd known how much pain you were in. Maybe I was too wrapped up in my own to realize what my kids needed."

"Dad, no. You were our rock. None of us would have survived the days after without you. Never doubt you were the best father we could have had."

"Thank you." Alex swallowed hard. "I wish I had a goddamned cigar," he muttered.

Aiden grinned. "Lizzie would have your head."

His father chuckled. "I'm a lucky man to have found two such amazing women in my life. Luckier still, none of you kids gave me a hard time about moving on."

"We just want you to be happy. And healthy," Aiden felt compelled to add.

"I want the same for all of you. Which brings us to the next thing you kept hidden."

He opened his eyes wide. "What's that?"

"Brooke."

He shook his head, knowing he couldn't talk about her. Not until he'd made things right.

Chapter Three

ON AIDEN'S FIRST day at Sterling Investments, he sat in a chair beside Jared in the main conference room. His brother was guiding Aiden in learning everything he needed to know about the company, and they'd hit the ground running. Though there was a lot to take in.

After a long morning session, Aiden stared out the glass window, startled when Brooke walked by, the sexy sway of her hips capturing his attention. Clenching his jaw, Aiden forced his stare back to the papers in front of him, but he inevitably took a peek at Brooke again, the see-through glass allowing him to track her progress down the hallway.

Considering she worked for the company and he, as acting CEO, was her superior, him watching her was beyond inappropriate. Which was a joke. She'd been employed here for a long time, and she knew more about his family's financial firm than he did.

At that thought, his gaze wandered again, and he got another glimpse of her, specifically her ass, just before she turned a corner and walked out of sight. Her narrow black skirt ended just above her knees, revealing her long, toned legs, and the sleek purple camisole with a V-neck that was driving him crazy.

Beside him, Jared cleared his throat.

Aiden straightened in his chair and returned his attention to where it belonged. But going over the finer points of the job Jared had been handling for years without a break already made Aiden dizzy.

"Hey. You seem to be having trouble focusing," Jared said, lifting an eyebrow with a *what's going on?* look.

"Sorry," he said, stifling a groan, and shoving thoughts of both Brooke, and other things, to the back of his mind.

Jared didn't know about their history. Aiden had kept their brief romantic past to himself, though clearly his father had sensed something emotional had happened between them. Brooke wasn't just an employee, she'd been part of their lives ever since Aiden's dad bought the mansion he still lived in, where Aiden was staying for now.

Brooke and her mother, Lizzie, had lived in the gatehouse and remained there as part of the original contract of sale for the main house. Lizzie had kept her job as the housekeeper, but they'd quickly become part of the Sterling family. All four of his siblings looked at Brooke like a sister, especially Fallon.

Aiden had once thought of her the same way, but

that changed when they were in college. He'd started to see her in a completely new light. A dark-haired temptation with the most gorgeous hazel eyes he'd ever seen. Despite the time that had passed since he'd held her in his arms, he was still drawn to her in ways he'd never felt for another woman.

Unfortunately, he'd burned that bridge. She wouldn't even look at him now.

Jared cleared his throat again.

Aiden had drifted off. Again. Shit. "I guess I just need a break. We've gone over a lot in the last couple of hours."

Jared nodded. "There's a lot to the job. Are you sure you're up for it?"

Aiden frowned. "Of course I am." He hoped he was telling the truth.

He'd majored in business because his father had always planned on him entering Sterling Investments, so he had the schooling required, but Aiden lacked the experience his brother had.

Jared eased back in his chair and eyed Aiden with a knowing gaze. "You don't just need a break from work. You're distracted. So, I've got to ask. We all know things between you and Brooke have been strained since you left and no one knows why. What's with you tracking her every move?"

Apparently, more people than Alex sensed something between them. But Aiden wouldn't go down without a fight.

"No, things haven't been strained, and you're imagining my staring. I'm just still jet-lagged."

Jared rolled his eyes. "Keep telling yourself that. I saw you watching her walk down the hall. I don't want to pry into your personal life, but I need to know you can handle working with her. Brooke is important to the company. In fact, she's one of our best executives."

"I'm aware." A swell of pride welled up inside him. She'd worked hard both through school and at proving herself here. "There's no reason we can't work together. I mean, come on. I've known her since I was fourteen and we get along just fine."

Gathering his papers and folders, Jared met his gaze. "You mean you used to get along."

"What's what supposed to mean?" Aiden asked. Now he sounded defensive. *Great.*

Jared rose to his feet, papers in hand. "You tiptoe around each other. Neither of you spend any real time together. It's like you're both trying to pretend things are fine without actually interacting."

"We—"

Jared held up one hand to stop him from speaking. "Don't bother coming up with an excuse. It's obvious to us all because you two used to be so close."

A pang of longing hit unexpectedly. Regret that he didn't want to face reared up inside of him and he did his best to keep his expression neutral. No point in giving Jared any ammunition to question him with.

"You've always brushed me off when I brought her up in the past, but I'd have to be blind to miss the looks you send her way when you think she's not looking. She does the same thing. It's been going on every time you've visited over the past few years."

At the thought of Brooke watching him, Aiden's heart squeezed in his chest, but he quickly shut down the flicker of hope that followed. She had every right to hate him after what he'd done, and he wouldn't allow himself to believe otherwise. That would just set him up to take a hard fall.

He didn't need that kind of pain.

Aiden stood, his laptop and cold coffee in hand. "You're wrong," he told his brother. "Brooke and I grew apart while I was gone, but that's normal. Now that I'm back for good, I'm sure we'll be friends again in no time."

A definite bold-faced lie.

But he didn't want to give Jared a reason to worry about the company once Charlie had the baby. His brother should be able to focus on his wife and daughter during his time off, and Aiden was determined not to let his past with Brooke get in the way of his ability to do the job.

A long moment of silence followed and finally, Jared nodded.

"How is Dad doing? We talked Friday night, but I don't have a good sense of his health yet," Aiden said, changing the subject. Working with their father, Jared had a front-row seat to Alex Sterling and Aiden wanted to catch up on how his dad was feeling.

Aiden flew in after his father's heart attack, and Alex had been pale and shaken. The worst part had been the dullness in his eyes, as if all life there had faded. It rattled Aiden to see his larger-than-life father so weak. His dad was the man with all the answers, the one who chased monsters out from under the bed when they were kids, and who held the family together after the grisly murder of their mom.

Aiden looked up to his remaining parent. Alex may have dominated in the boardroom but as a father, he was always there, supporting his kids and their dreams. In Aiden's mind, his dad was ageless and invincible.

"He's grumpy," Jared said.

"No doubt because of all the adjustments Lizzie is enforcing."

His brother nodded. "The doctors aren't letting him off with a warning this time. They're demanding he follow their regimen. A heart-healthy diet, daily cholesterol meds, and even an exercise program."

Aiden couldn't help but chuckle as he imagined his father's reaction. Alex Sterling was a stubborn man, and he didn't like being told what to do. But while the first heart attack had been minor, this second one was worse, and had included surgery and a prolonged hospital stay, scaring them all.

"You know him. Never show weakness." Jared continued. "Honestly, I'm hoping we can convince him to officially retire."

Aiden grimaced. "I don't know if he'll go for that. You know how dedicated he is to this place."

"Oh, I know. After the first heart attack, he was supposed to slow down, but he still spent way too much time here." Jared's head tilted to the side as he studied Aiden. "Actually, you seemed to have a similar mindset about your job until recently. Not that I'm complaining. I'm glad you're back. It makes me feel a lot more comfortable taking time off."

Aiden forced a grin. "Happy to help," he said. What he didn't disclose was that the timing worked out well.

He'd needed to take a step back from his occupation as a journalist. A familiar unease settled in the pit of his stomach as he recalled the danger that found him, courtesy of his most recent planned article. Trouble wasn't unusual in his line of work. Hell, he'd been in a vehicle too damned close to an IED once.

But this situation was different. He could feel it deep in his gut. "I just needed a change and your time off coincided with that," Aiden said, shifting the laptop tucked beneath his arm. "Why don't we meet up again after lunch? Your little one will be here before we know it, so we'd better pack in my tutoring while we can."

Jared nodded. "Sounds good."

They walked out, Jared discussing their afternoon plans to go over the company's assets, liabilities, and equity. Keeping busy with thoughts of Sterling Investments made it easier to push aside thinking about Brooke and the danger from his latest job.

The future of the company relied on Aiden for now, and he was determined not to let his family down.

Chapter Four

Brooke had seen Aiden watching her. She'd felt his gaze following her path down the hallway, as if such a thing were possible. And though she hated to admit it, she'd dressed for his return.

Her feet were sore since she had on heels two inches higher than she normally wore to the office, but she'd felt compelled to slip into the sexiest pair of shoes she owned. The ones that made her legs look a mile long and did amazing things for her ass.

As she stood at the elevator, pressing the DOWN button and waiting for the lift to come back up from the ground floor, she chided herself for caring. She'd never thought much about what outfit she'd wear until the morning of Aiden's first day of work.

She had a whole closet full of business casual clothes and sensible low heels, as she preferred her outfits professional and comfortable. In fact, she'd had to dig in the back of her closet to find these damn sexy heels today. And she *might* have spent a little extra time trying to perfect a smokey eye that matched the plum camisole she'd chosen.

She'd dressed with him in mind, a small part of her

hoping he'd notice the extra effort she put into her appearance. She wanted him to eat his heart out, to regret ever hurting and leaving her. Petty? Maybe. True? Absolutely.

Irritated with herself, she let out a huff and shifted her weight, silently willing the elevator to come faster. It was certainly taking its time getting to the tenth floor, and all Brooke wanted to do was get home and soak herself in a hot tub. She might even crack open a bottle of wine. Maybe that would help her forget about the way Aiden's proximity was affecting her.

Since early this morning, she'd avoided him but after lunch, she'd seen him often. Every time they made accidental eye contact, her heart lurched. When she caught a whiff of his cologne, the same scent he'd always worn, memories swept over her.

Their past had haunted her for too damned long, had impacted every date she'd had, and lately, she'd been telling herself it was time to put it, and him, behind her. Then, when Alex's health declined and Aiden returned to the city, she was back to being obsessive and emotional over him. It was infuriating.

Light feminine laughter sounded from behind her and Brooke glanced over her shoulder. Two familiar women walked toward her, Lisa, an analyst, and Madison who worked in the treasury department. They were close friends, and Brooke got along well with them, although she considered them to be more colleagues than anything else.

Madison nodded at her in acknowledgement, but Lisa was too busy talking to notice Brooke at all. It didn't bother her. The woman was well-known for spreading gossip around the workplace.

They paused behind her. "I heard that he's single," Lisa said. "It's kind of hard to believe, considering how good-looking he is."

"That's what you used to say about his brother," Madison mused.

Lisa chuckled. "Yeah, but now Jared's married and off the market. Aiden, however…"

At her words, Brooke's stomach twisted in tight knots. It shouldn't strike her as odd that Aiden was the subject of office gossip, but Brooke didn't want to hear what other women had to say about him. Even more, she didn't want to care. But she was stuck waiting for the elevator, which always took forever at the end of the day. And she wasn't about to take the stairs and walk down ten floors in the stupid heels.

"He *is* hot," Madison agreed.

They'd moved so they were standing beside Brooke, but she kept her gaze locked on the elevator doors. She could see her own hazy reflection in the metal.

"And you know he's rich since he's a Sterling," Lisa said. "Whoever lands him is going to be one lucky woman."

Unable to stop herself, Brooke turned to face the two women. Hands on her hips, she stared down Madison first, then Lisa.

Their eyes opened wide, both obviously startled. It would be better to bury her emotions and not say a word, but she disliked hearing these women objectify Aiden.

Brooke's feelings for him were complicated, but before she fell for him, he'd been one of her best friends. "You know, there's more to a man than looks and money."

The women stared at her.

"And those are probably the least important things about Aiden. He's a *person* with feelings." She knew even more. He'd volunteered at a soup kitchen once a week during college. He was a huge Mets fan and loved Hawaiian pizza. *And* he'd taught himself how to play the drums when he was just a teenager. "Any woman that wants Aiden Sterling needs to appreciate *all* the things about him, not just his fat bank account," she informed the two stunned employees.

Madison's mouth had dropped open. Clearly, she was surprised at her outburst.

"Just how well do you know him?" Lisa asked, and Brooke immediately realized her mistake.

Her friendship with Jared wasn't a secret, but she didn't share her long, personal history with the Sterling family around the office. She didn't want anyone to think she was given special treatment or didn't deserve her position in the company. She'd *earned* her spot as an executive with Sterling Investments. Starting with an internship during college, she'd worked her way up in the firm and was now one of the top executives.

The doors finally opened, and she turned away from Madison and Lisa, and stepped into the elevator without answering the question.

Unfortunately, they were also leaving for the day, so they rode down with her. The air was thick with tension.

"We didn't mean anything by it," Madison, the sweeter of the two, said to Brooke as the doors opened.

"I know. You just don't want the wrong person to overhear you gossiping." She spoke as a company executive. But as a woman, she added, "And it's not a bad thing to remember looks aren't everything." She paused, then wanting to break the ice, she said, "But it doesn't hurt, either."

Madison let out a relieved breath and Lisa laughed.

"But point taken," Madison said. "It won't happen again."

Brooke nodded. Neither woman needed to know

she'd been defending the man who'd broken her heart.

The elevator doors opened. "Good night," she said, as she stepped out and strode across the marble floor. She exited the building through the glass doors that led to the parking lot and headed home.

Chapter Five

AIDEN ARRIVED HOME and immediately glanced toward the gatehouse before pulling into the garage. Habit had him looking to see if Brooke's little blue PT Cruiser was parked in front of the gatehouse. It was and he was glad. Though he hadn't gone out of his way to interact with her, giving her space, he liked knowing she was around. He took bittersweet comfort in the fact that he was closer to her now than he had been in years.

He walked into his childhood home through the garage entrance, passing through a mudroom and into the kitchen. The place was immaculate, the granite countertops gleaming under the recessed lighting and not a speck of dirt on the floors. Lizzie kept the house pristine and as she was now dating his dad, the line between employee and girlfriend had blurred.

Aiden headed for the foyer, intending to go to his bedroom, but restless energy had him pivoting and heading out the front door. He didn't have a destination in mind as he walked, he just wanted to stretch his legs and breathe some fresh air. Coming home had been the right thing to do but he hadn't acclimated to the easier pace yet.

The family estate was sprawling, the lawn perfectly manicured, trees lining the edge of the property. He walked at a leisurely pace, enjoying the sunshine on his face, when movement at the gatehouse caught his eye.

Brooke stepped out of the house and onto the little covered porch, turning to pull the door closed behind her. A pair of jeans hugged her hips and delectable ass, and she'd taken down the short ponytail she'd worn to work.

His fingers itched to touch her, the memory of their one night together fresh in his mind. Everything inside him was drawn to her, and not just in a physical way. He missed hearing her laugh and watching her hands fly around as she gestured when telling a story. He missed the smell of the coconut shampoo that always lingered on her hair.

Most of all, he missed wrapping his arms around her waist.

Suddenly fed up with this avoidance game, he changed directions and headed her way. Brooke had just sat down on the porch step when she spotted him. She tensed and, based on the way her eyes darted to the front door, he had no doubt she contemplated heading back inside before he could reach her.

He picked up his pace, closing the distance between them before she made a decision.

Standing before her, he met her wary gaze. "Hi, Brooke."

"Hello, Aiden." She remained seated. "What brings you by?" she asked, her fingers curling around the bluestone step.

"We need to talk."

She tilted her head to the side and crossed her arms over her chest, lips thinned and eyes narrowed. "We don't have anything to discuss," she said, coolly.

"I beg to differ. We can't keep avoiding each other at work and I'd rather our first confrontation be in private."

"At least you know it's going to be a confrontation," she muttered. She rose to her feet and stepped down so she was on the path beside him.

He appreciated both her honesty and her ability to face him with justified anger. "Are you ever going to forgive me for leaving?" he asked.

Hurt flashed in her hazel eyes before she banked all emotion. "You know there's more to it than that. And let's face it, you have to be sorry in order to be forgiven."

He scrubbed a hand over his face and groaned. She had a point. He'd never apologized for his actions. He couldn't bring himself to say *I'm sorry*, because even after all this time, he believed that breaking her heart had been the right choice. It made him an asshole, but he'd learned to live with it.

At least he'd known that while he was gone traveling the world and throwing himself into work, she'd been able to go on with her life and not sit around waiting for the times he *might* be able to come home. But with her standing in front of him, pissed off and hurt, he second-guessed his reasoning and the weight of his decision lay heavy on his shoulders.

Those were all excuses that made things easier for him to live with. Not her. She deserved the apology but apparently, he'd waited too long because Brooke rolled her eyes and turned away, marching back up the three steps to her front door.

Fuck.

Instinct had him following her and grabbing her wrist. He spun her around and pressed her back against the wall beside the door. Leaning his body against hers, he bit back a groan at the feeling of her soft curves pressed against his harder ones. Desire raged through his bloodstream, and his cock hardened in his slacks.

She met his gaze with guarded eyes, but inside the green, gold, and brown depths he saw the fire raging inside of her. Anger and desire. He understood the latter well. She still wanted him. She might not be happy about it, but she couldn't hide the truth.

Brushing a strand of hair behind her ear, he trailed

his fingertips down her jaw, feeling the silkiness of her skin.

Her lips parted as she dragged in a shaky breath, and he rubbed his thumb over her plump bottom lip. She wasn't wearing makeup anymore, but she was still gorgeous.

Her eyes darkened with need. With her face inches from his, he longed to close the distance and press their mouths together in a heated kiss. He was so damn *hungry* for her.

"Do you ever think about our night together?" he asked, his tone gruff.

"No." But her voice trembled.

"Don't lie to me, Brooke."

Her cheeks turned red and he couldn't hold back a grin. He'd always been able to tell when she was lying, and now was no different. "There you go," he murmured. "Your flushed skin gives you away."

She pulled her bottom lip between her teeth and released it. "Dammit."

He chuckled, moving his hands to her hips. Her palms were already on his chest, fisting his shirt, although whether that was to pull him closer or push him away remained to be seen.

He had no doubt she was conflicted because despite the distance, both physical and emotional, Aiden *knew* her. She wanted him, but she was still pissed off, too.

He wouldn't push her but he *would* remind her. "I don't just recall that night," he said, giving her hips a light squeeze. "I think about it *all the time.*"

Her breath hitched at the same time she shook her head in denial. "No," she said. "You don't. *You can't.*"

"Are you trying to convince me of that? Or yourself?" he asked. "Because I still remember the way you felt… And the little whimper you made when I sank deep inside you."

Her grip on his shirt tightened and her mouth parted in a soft gasp. But she flattened her palms on his chest and shoved him away… all without warning. She wasn't strong enough to move him, though he took the hint, stepping back.

"Don't do that again," she snapped, turning to the door. "Just leave me alone, Aiden."

The sadness in her voice hit him like a punch to the gut. No matter how much he wanted to call her back, he respected her need to walk away.

She unlocked her door and stepped inside, her eyes locking with his briefly before she slammed the door. The sound of the deadbolt drove her point home. He wasn't welcome.

Shoving his hands in his pockets, he turned away and walked back to the main house. He took comfort in the not-so-small fact that despite her hurt, she still seemed to want him, giving him something to work with. He'd given up on the idea of being with her once, and it had been the biggest mistake of his life.

No matter what she believed, Brooke Snyder was meant to be his. He'd been kidding himself to think otherwise.

Chapter Six

Brooke slammed the door on Aiden and what had to be his lies. How could he claim to remember every moment of their time together when he'd dumped her so easily the next day? And how could she physically respond so quickly to him after all the years of pain he'd caused her?

Grrr.

Brooke stalked to the kitchen and poured herself a glass of much-needed wine. Leaning against the counter, she took a long sip and did her best to calm down. Once she felt better, she headed for her bedroom and placed the glass on the nightstand.

Then, despite her common sense, she opened the closet, lifted on her tiptoes, and grabbed a box from the high shelf. Taking the treasured item to the bed, she opened the top and lifted out the first scrapbook she'd ever made.

She'd been twenty years old, having a blast in college, and wanted to document every experience she had. Since then, she'd created multiple volumes, and she loved looking through them to revisit her favorite memories. To this day, the books were lined up on a shelf in her room. This first one was the only album she kept tucked away because the memories inside hurt so badly.

Flipping it open, she stared at a picture of herself, Fallon and Aiden sitting on a bench she remembered being in a park near their home. The siblings smiled broadly with their heads leaned in toward Brooke in the middle. They'd been so happy, and Brooke's chest felt tight as she looked at the photo, remembering that day.

There had been a concert in the park and Aiden had been protective of both her and Fallon, keeping a close eye on them as they danced to the music. She smiled as she recalled him forcing them to drink water often and glaring at any man that approached. At the time, he'd probably considered her to be like a sister, no different than Fallon.

But Brooke had allowed herself to pretend there'd been more, that he'd felt protective and possessive because he shared her feelings. She'd been falling in love with him even then.

Maybe she'd *always* loved him.

She continued to flip through the pages. Aiden was featured on so many. Sometimes the two of them were with Fallon, or other friends at parties or dinners. Other times they were hanging around campus. On occasion, it had been just the two of them.

They'd both studied business, so they often crammed for tests together or he'd guide her when she wrote her papers. Aiden was older, further along in his studies, and she'd been grateful for his help. Things between them changed that year. They'd grown closer and she could see the progression of *them* as she neared the end of the scrapbook.

The last picture in the book showed the two of them at his college graduation. She'd been so proud, and she could see the joy in her face. Aiden stood, handsome in his cap and gown, with his entire future ahead of him.

He'd slung his arm around her shoulders and hope flared to life when he pulled her to him. Though they were just posing for a photo, the moment felt intimate. Afterward, he didn't move away. Despite being surrounded by his family, he'd kept her tucked into his side longer than necessary.

She'd looked at him then, their faces so close, and there'd been a spark in his eyes, a warmth that made her believe he finally saw her as more than a friend, or an unofficial family member. She had no idea he'd already made up his mind. He was in the process of making moves to become a traveling journalist and leave New York. A few short weeks later, he'd destroyed her hope for their future.

Slamming the scrapbook closed, Brooke gulped

down the last swallow of her red wine and put the book away. There was no use living in the past.

Chapter Seven

AIDEN HAD A meeting with his editor, and he was late. John would be handling the article due out soon, just as he had all Aiden's other journalistic pieces. The older man had chosen a coffee shop thirty minutes from Sterling Investments and despite the app telling him exactly what time he'd arrive, there'd been an accident on the way holding up traffic.

He jogged to the entrance and glanced around the outdoor seats. John had snagged a table on the patio, and Aiden nodded his head at him before heading inside to order coffee. The rich smell of roasted beans filled the air, along with the indistinguishable buzz of voices mixed together.

Luckily, there wasn't a line. Most people were already seated with their drinks. After ordering a large mocha latte, he moved to the end of the counter. While waiting, he studied the black-and-white framed photos on the walls featuring various scenes throughout the city.

Suddenly, a tingle of awareness sizzled down his spine. He'd been on enough assignments to be aware when someone was watching him, and he had that feeling now. He turned around, scanning the shop and the patrons inside, but no one stood out or quickly looked away. Next, he glanced out the front window, but he didn't see anyone watching him there, either.

The barista called out his name and the sensation passed, but Aiden was still on edge. He picked up his drink and strode outside, settling in on a hard metal chair across from his editor. Looking around, he knew why John had picked the place. The tables were placed far enough apart to make it unlikely their conversation would be overheard.

"Sorry I'm late," Aiden said, easing back into his seat.

"Don't worry about it." John pushed his wire-framed glasses up his nose. "I'm just enjoying some time out of the office. My doctor's been telling me I spend too many hours hunched over the keyboard and staring at a computer screen. It makes my wife happy if I listen to him."

Aiden chuckled, the man's words reminding him of his father and Lizzie.

"One day you'll get married and know what I mean," John said, laughing.

With the way Brooke avoided him, Aiden doubted it. And he couldn't see himself growing older with anyone but her. He merely shook his head, causing John to grin.

In his mid-fifties, John Hall had worked for decades at the global online and print magazine that employed both him and Aiden. John was well-respected in the world of journalism, and Aiden had learned a lot from him, and considered John his mentor.

Aiden took a sip of his drink, enjoying the chocolate flavor. "So, do you have a timeline for when my article will run?"

"Three weeks. Front page of the next issue." John braced his arms on the table and leaned in. "Are you sure you want it to be your last? I understand you need a break to help with your family's business, but this article is your best piece yet, and I think it'll make your career. There's no reason you can't return in a few months when things settle at home."

Aiden groaned and ran his fingers through his hair. The article *was* good. He knew that. It was also the reason he'd decided to make this piece his last.

"I don't think I'm finished with journalism, but I can't see myself going back to the traveling aspect of this job. I miss having a home base." He missed his family and most of all, he missed Brooke.

"Is that the only reason you want to step back?" John asked.

No, Aiden thought. There was more. The job had started off simple enough. He'd been sent to a small

European country to investigate rumors of misuse of government funds. Despite the tip-off, Aiden had expected to discover the claims were unfounded.

But a few months in, he had uncovered embezzlement of reserve funds in a country that was already dealing with political unrest. The person, or persons, behind the corruption was still unknown but the proof Aiden discovered was enough to make someone nervous enough to commit murder.

"You already know Ingrid was killed," Aiden whispered to John. "I can't say I enjoyed being a target." The danger during this last assignment had been unexpected and worse than the near miss with the IED.

"I know," he said sadly.

Ingrid had been Aiden's best source in the Government Finance Officers Association. Part of her job at the GFOA had been to provide guidelines for the government's financial management. Her position allowed her access that proved misappropriation of the reserve funds. Aiden had been sure that he could use what she uncovered to nail who was behind the corruption.

"After she died, there were people watching me all the time, secret surveillance, people ransacking my room, and open threats." He'd been jumping at shadows and meeting government employees in secret to compile information.

John nodded. "But you stuck with it until you uncovered the truth."

"Part of the truth," Aiden said. "And that came at too heavy a cost." Ingrid had gone missing after one of their meetings and a short time later, Aiden had been sent a picture of her body before she'd been discovered days later, with no evidence leading to the culprit.

Scrawled on the back of the photo had been a simple demand.

STOP DIGGING.

His stomach churned at the memory.

Knowing he'd come to a dead end, he'd spoken to John, and they agreed he should leave the country. But Aiden refused to sit on the information. He had a duty as a journalist to share the facts with the world. Not to mention failing to report on the corruption would make Ingrid's sacrifice for nothing.

But the threats didn't stop when he returned home. "I got a note this week," he said, leaning forward and lowering his voice again. "It was put in my luggage, which tells me these people have access at high levels."

John frowned. "What did it say?"

"Kill the story. Or else." Aiden ran a hand through

his hair as John muttered a curse. "I recognized the handwriting. It was the same bastards who killed Ingrid. She was easy prey, but they've made it clear they'll come for me, too, if we run the story."

John reset his glasses on his nose. "Are you saying you want me to pull it?"

Aiden shook his head. "No. But this is it for me. I'm ready to move on to something new." He didn't think working corporate at the family business was his calling for the future, but he had time to figure out his next steps.

"I get it. I did the traveling thing for a few years in my early days too, and it's rough. Add in some unhinged bastard sending you threats, and I can't blame you for taking a step back." John took a sip of his coffee. "Just know you always have a job with us."

Aiden smiled. "Thank you."

"As for the threat, I'd say report it if you want to—"

"No. We need the article to run first and expose the bastards." Besides, going to the police seemed pointless when the threat was vague; he had no proof who was responsible for Ingrid's death, which had happened on foreign soil. "All I can do right now is stay vigilant and hope the danger passes once the article runs. I can't see the police here being able to do much about something that happened so far away."

John inclined his head. "Fine. Then be on the lookout for trouble and be careful. But I don't think they'll come for you here in the U.S. If the story triggers an investigation into the corruption, whoever is after you will have much bigger problems than a reporter who pissed them off."

"I wish I was that confident," Aiden muttered, a shudder rushing through him.

They finished their drinks, talking about some of his best articles. John told him about his upcoming plans for the magazine, and Aiden sensed he was still trying to tempt him to return.

It wasn't going to work.

Chapter Eight

"WHO IS THE cutest baby in the whole wide world?" Brooke cooed as she lifted Fallon's chubby one-month-old baby into her arms. They sat in Fallon's bright white kitchen, each on chairs at the table.

Girls abounded in the Sterling family and Fallon was no different. Gabriella, Gabbi for short, stared up at her with big, blue eyes. She hadn't started smiling yet, which made her seem like such a serious little girl.

Grasping for Brooke's face, the baby tried to reach for her nose and missed.

Fallon laughed.

"I warned you," Fallon said, opening a bottle of water and taking a long sip. "She's trying to touch anything she can get her hands on."

"Gabbi is just curious, aren't you, baby girl?" Brooke ran her finger down the infant's soft cheek. She'd come to Fallon's new house after work, wanting to check on her and see her bundle of joy.

Her best friend had given birth a month ago, but she looked great. Of course she had dark circles under her eyes, courtesy of sleepless nights, but Fallon was thrilled to have her baby here at last.

"How are you doing?" Brooke asked, reaching out to grab a cookie from the white cardboard box on the kitchen table. Knowing Fallon had a sweet tooth, Brooke had brought an assortment of treats from her favorite bakery.

"I'm good," Fallon said, smiling fondly at Gabbi. "It's just amazing how tired I am, considering that all this lovebug does is eat and sleep."

Brooke laughed. "How often does she wake up?"

"Every couple of hours. Noah tries to help with her as much as possible, but he can't help with the feedings, and that's what keeps me up at night."

Brooke laughed. "Yeah, it's too bad men can't breastfeed. Where is he now?"

Smiling, Fallon said, "He took the twins to the park. The girls are over staring at a newborn who does nothing but sleep and burp, according to Dylan." She grinned when speaking of her stepdaughters, her husband's twins from a prior... well, Brooke would say relationship, but it had actually been a one-night stand.

Noah split custody with his ex, Charlie, who happened to be married to Jared Sterling now. Since they were also expecting a baby soon, the twins were about to have another little half-sibling. The Sterling family kept expanding.

"They're great with her, but they've already realized that babies can be boring. Dylan can't wait until she's older and more *fashionable*. Her new thing is that she wants to become a fashion designer, so I have a feeling that Gabbi has a ton of outrageous outfits to look forward to wearing."

"Until she changes her mind and wants to become something else. What about Dakota?" Brooke asked about Dylan's twin.

"You know her, obsessed with facts about archaeology. She's already planning to teach the baby all she knows."

Dakota's interest in archaeology came from Charlie, her mom, who had spent time on a dig overseas and now worked in a museum. The girl was eleven years old and talked about death all the time, but in a factual way, sharing morbid information about ancient civilizations and how they performed their burials, how scientists used bones to learn about their owner's lifestyle, or how human skin shrunk after death.

That last one had been explained while Brooke was trying to eat fried chicken, and her stomach hadn't been able to handle that particular food ever since. "Well, I supposed it's nice that she wants to connect with her baby sister that way," Brooke said.

Fallon laughed. "Don't worry. We'll be having some talks about what is age-appropriate before Gabbi is old enough to be traumatized."

They hung out for the next half hour, chatting about everything and nothing.

Fallon confirmed that she was recovering well from childbirth, but she leaned forward with a grin. "I have to admit I'm happy that the six-week mark and getting clearance to have sex again is around the corner. No one ever told me how attractive fatherhood can look on a guy that steps up and takes care of his baby. It's kind of driving me crazy that I have to wait."

Brooke shook her head. "Must be nice to have a man that you want so badly."

Fallon placed a hand on her arm. "I'm sorry. I didn't mean to rub your face in my happy relationship."

"I didn't mean it that way, and I wouldn't want you to walk on eggshells around me just because I'm hopelessly single." Brooke's thoughts went to Aiden, who she'd seen in the office today. He'd treated her to a simple wink and her panties had been soaked through.

Fallon frowned. "There's no one that you're interested in? Maybe someone at the office or your gym?"

"No," Brooke said, even as her mind conjured up the heated look in Aiden's eyes last night when he'd pinned her against the wall on her front porch.

"There's no one I feel a connection with."

"Is it possible you're being too picky? I mean, you don't have to feel insta-love with a guy to have a little fun. Scratch that itch, girl. It's been a while, hasn't it?"

Way too long, Brooke thought. But Fallon had always been more of a free spirit than she was. It was part of what made their friendship work so well. They complemented each other with their differences.

"I don't know that I'm really the type to have casual sex. I want to at least be attracted to and like a guy before we sleep together."

Fallon tapped her finger against her cheek, looking thoughtful. "Are you *sure* there's *no one* you're interested in?" she asked again, this time more pointedly.

Brooke knew exactly what her friend was implying. Everything came back to Aiden.

Fallon wasn't stupid. Despite Brooke's silence on the subject, she'd been with Brooke and Aiden at college while they'd grown close. Fallon had even asked what was going on between Brooke and her brother, leading Brooke to admit she had feelings for Aiden.

But that had been before *that night* and his breakup—if she could call it that—the next day. Since then, Brooke refused to talk about Aiden at all. When Fallon mentioned him, Brooke changed the subject. But Fallon had to know that *something* occurred to turn

Brooke against her brother. She just never pushed, respecting Brooke's boundaries.

"Nope. There's no one I want to be with," Brooke said. Lying to her friend felt wrong, but Brooke was starting to realize she'd been lying to herself about her feelings for Aiden, so what difference did it make?

"Okay, but I worry about you. You rarely date, which wouldn't be a problem, but sometimes you seem so lonely."

Brooke winced. Fallon's blunt honesty was the kind that only a good friend would give, but it still hurt to hear.

"I'm not lonely…" she started to say, but trailed off at the no-nonsense look in Fallon's eyes. Brooke couldn't bullshit her. "Okay, I'm lonely. I mean, I have friends and coworkers. I have my mom. And my career is important to me. I have a pretty full life. But lately, it seems like everyone around me is in a happy, fulfilling relationship, and I just wish I had that too."

Fallon touched Brooke's hand, which still held the baby. "You deserve it."

Brooke nodded, doing her best not to let tears well as she spoke. "I want to come home to someone that can't wait to see me, and who wants to spend time with me. I want to feel a warm, masculine body pressed against me in bed at night and wake up to someone's smiling face in the morning."

The *someone* in her mind was Aiden, and she hated that she couldn't get him out of her thoughts and dreams. After all this time, she should be over him.

Fallon's eyes softened. "That's beautiful, Brooke. I really want that for you."

"I'm sure I'll meet someone eventually." She looked down at the infant in her arms and lowered her voice. "I think she's asleep." The subject change was deliberate.

Fallon stood and carefully took Gabbi from her arms without waking her up. Brooke followed her down the hall, opening the door to the nursery. The room was dimly lit by a nightlight, but Brooke could make out the various animals painted on the walls. An elephant, a giraffe, monkeys in trees, and birds flying near the ceiling. Fallon was an amazing artist, and she'd painted all this herself.

Brooke lingered in the doorway, watching as Fallon crossed to the wooden crib and slowly placed Gabbi on her back. Turning on the mobile, which had bunnies hanging down over her, Fallon silently tiptoed back to Brooke and slowly closed the door behind them.

A pang of longing hit her unexpectedly. In all her musings, she'd never thought about wanting kids. Of course she did, someday, but this was the first time she felt that biological urge. Did she see herself having a family or did the specter of Aiden linger and shut down that hope? Because she couldn't envision the scenario with anyone else.

Once back in the hallway, Fallon let out a relieved breath. "Let's go to the living room." They settled side by side on the comfortable sofa. "Thank God she's finally getting used to sleeping in the crib," Fallon said.

"I bet."

Fallon met her gaze. "I'm so glad you came to visit. I've missed you. Besides, I have something to ask. I don't know if you'll agree but now that you've admitted you're not interested in anyone, I hope you'll keep an open mind."

"About what?" Brooke asked warily.

Pulling her phone out of her back pocket, Fallon opened her photo gallery and held it out for Brooke to see. A man with dark eyes and dirty blond hair cut short on the sides and longer on top stared back. He had a clean-shaven jaw and a dimple in his chin.

"He's cute, right?" Fallon asked.

Brooke raised one eyebrow. "You do remember that you're married, right?"

Fallon slapped her arm playfully. "He's for you. His name is Mark and he's a lawyer from Noah's firm. I want to set you up with him."

Oh, no. But before Brooke could reply, the front door opened, and Fallon's husband, Noah, walked inside. The twins weren't with him, so Brooke figured they'd been dropped off at Charlie and Jared's house.

"Hey, sweetheart," he said, coming into the living room and going straight to Fallon. He pressed a kiss to her lips before turning. "Hi, Brooke. How are you?"

She smiled. "I'm good, thanks. And you?"

His grin told the story. "Great. Is Gabbi napping?" he asked his wife.

"Yeah, she just went down," Fallon said. "And I was showing Brooke a picture of Mark."

Noah glanced at the screen and shook his head, a frown on his handsome face. "I don't like that you have his picture on your phone."

Fallen rolled her eyes. "Maybe I'll make it my wallpaper so that I have something pretty to look at."

He let out a growl-like noise, and Brooke snickered. These two had the kind of teasing relationship anyone would aspire to.

While Fallon and Noah talked, Brooke thought about Fallon's suggestion. She'd been planning on turning down the blind date, hating the idea of an awkward night full of forced small talk. But watching her friend and her husband, Brooke decided to take a chance and say yes instead.

What harm could it do? Maybe it wouldn't work out, but *maybe* it would. Maybe she'd end up with their kind of relationship, one full of love and respect. She wanted a man to look at her the way Noah looked at Fallon. She wanted to glow with happiness the way her friend did.

For that to happen, she had to put herself out there. She had to forget about the infuriating man she'd loved for what seemed like forever. She'd been comparing every guy she dated to Aiden since even before they got together. It wasn't fair to her potential boyfriends *or* to her.

Nor did it help that Aiden had returned and she was forced to see him at work. That he'd cornered her outside her home and brought up the night they'd slept together. She wanted him so much that her entire body had tingled at the memory, but she couldn't go there again.

She had to move on.

"Okay," Brooke said. "I'll go on a date with him."

Fallon's jaw dropped, her mouth open wide. "You will?"

Brooke couldn't help but laugh. "You seem surprised."

"I am. I thought I'd have to try harder to talk you into it."

Noah listened to them, his smile wide. "I'm going to check on the baby. Good to see you, Brooke." Noah started for the hallway.

"Don't you dare pick her up!" Fallon called after

him, but she immediately turned back to Brooke. "So, what changed your mind? I know you were going to say no."

"I guess I'm ready to try something new." Brooke shrugged like it was no big deal, but she knew it was. "When can I meet him?"

"How does Friday night sound, if he's free?" Fallon asked.

That seemed soon, but why not? She wouldn't have time to talk herself out of it.

"Make it happen," Brooke said with more confidence than she felt.

She stayed for a little longer and they chatted about what she should wear to dinner with Mark. She was already nervous about the date but also tentatively excited. It felt good to be moving forward instead of being stuck in the past.

As she walked into the gatehouse later, her thoughts were wrapped up in the possibility of hitting things off with the handsome lawyer. A light shone from the kitchen, so she assumed her mom was home.

"I'm back," she called out from the front door as she kicked off her shoes. "And I brought some treats from Posh Bakery."

She walked toward the kitchen with the box in her hands and a smile on her face, but instead of her mother, Aiden stood at the kitchen sink and looked at her over his shoulder.

She paused in the entryway, surprised to see him in her home.

"Posh Bakery, huh? I forgot all about that place. They had the *best* snickerdoodles."

His sexy grin caused her heart to beat faster. "What are you doing here?" she asked, as she stepped into the room and placed the box on the counter.

He lifted a wrench in his hand. "The garbage disposal stopped working this morning and your mom asked me to come by and take a look."

Her gaze shifted past him, and she saw water filling the sink and a toolbox on the floor. "Thanks for helping out my mom, but I can hire someone to handle it."

The last thing she needed was for him to have an excuse to be in her home, in her space.

"I can't do that," he said. "I promised your mother I'd help." He eased down on his knees in front of the sink.

She ground her teeth together, frustrated with him, his presence, and with herself. "Just *go*, Aiden. Leaving is what you're good at, after all." On edge, she spoke before she could stop herself.

He flinched and she regretted her impulsive words. She wasn't mean. In fact, she'd never spoken so harshly to Aiden or anyone else, not even the night he broke her heart. These tumultuous emotions were turning her into someone she didn't recognize or like.

He stood and turned on the water. Flicking on the garbage disposal, the sound of it running filled the otherwise silent kitchen and he nodded to himself.

"I just had to push the reset button on the bottom," he said, as he turned it back off. "I didn't want you to waste money on something I could fix."

Her chest squeezed tight at his thoughtfulness. "Aiden, look, I didn't mean that the way it came out."

"It's fine." He picked up his toolbox and started for the door.

"Aiden—"

"It's okay, Brooke. Really," he said, and walked out of the gatehouse without looking back.

Alone in the kitchen, she stared at the closed door, her insides feeling as if they'd been scooped out, leaving her empty. She wouldn't have thought that anything could be worse than the anger and hurt she'd been carrying around, but this hollow feeling trumped it. And *that* was the reason she needed to go on that date. It was about more than finding a man to love. It was about healing, for both her and Aiden.

All this time, she believed she was the only one hurting. After all, he was the one who'd left. But she now understood they were both in pain, and it didn't have to be that way. If she let go of the anger that had become her natural response to Aiden over the years, then perhaps he could too. They could both be happy.

They might even become friends again.

Finding a new normal would take work, but if she managed it, she could have one of her best friends back in her life. It would be like the night they spent together never happened.

Chapter Nine

AIDEN MADE IT through his first week at Sterling Investments and he was grateful it was Friday. After work, he returned to his father's house. Eventually, he'd start looking for his own place, but for now he was enjoying being home.

He sat at the kitchen island, checking his emails and responding to work colleagues, when Lizzie walked into the kitchen, humming.

"Hi, Lizzie."

"Hello, Aiden. How was your day?" she asked, as she went to the refrigerator and began pulling out ingredients to make dinner.

Aiden grinned as he saw the salmon. "Good, but I'm glad this first week is behind me. So, salmon, huh?"

She laughed. "He'll eat it and he won't complain."

His dad, a big fan of red meat, was not going to be thrilled with any heart-healthy meal. But Lizzie was right. He'd eat it anyway. He didn't talk much about the heart attack—aside from complaining about his dietary restrictions and daily exercises—but Aiden knew the last attack had scared him, proven by how he now followed doctor's orders and Lizzie's demands.

"I should get out of your way." Aiden closed his laptop and started to slide off his stool, but Lizzie gestured for him to stop.

"Please, stay. I could use the company."

Happy to spend time with her, Aiden settled back and watched as Lizzie pulled out a variety of vegetables from the refrigerator and pantry.

"How are you settling in?" she asked, and began to mix herbs and lemon juice as a sauce. "Is it boring after all your exciting travels?"

Aiden thought about the danger he was still facing from his last assignment. "Sometimes excitement is overrated."

"Well, I hope that means you're here to stay, even after Jared's paternity leave is over. You've been missed." Pausing in her meal prep, she looked directly at him with hazel eyes so similar to Brooke's. "There's a lot of love for you around here, Aiden."

He grinned. "Yeah, I know. I'm pretty damn lucky to have such a great family."

Reaching across the island, she placed a hand on his and gave it a squeeze. "Yes, you do. But they aren't the only ones who care."

Something significant passed between them at those words, and Aiden knew Lizzie had been referring to Brooke. Whether she'd told her mother about them, he didn't know, but he doubted it. Brooke had been the one to suggest they keep their situation quiet, but he'd come to realize his family members knew something was up.

And a mother didn't always have to be told things to sense them. Thinking back to his own mom, he recalled how intuitive she'd been about her kids' thoughts and feelings. His lips curved at the memory. She'd been a great mother and they'd lost her too soon.

A sudden realization hit him. He hadn't just been running from guilt. He hadn't wanted to face the empty feeling he'd carried with him. If he wasn't home, he wouldn't have as much time to think about her, to remember the loss. But that, too, stayed with him abroad.

Lizzie had gone back to working on dinner, placing the salmon on a baking sheet and putting it into the oven.

"What else are you making?" he asked her.

"Along with the salmon, a shredded vegetable salad and brown rice. Your father's going to hate it."

Aiden laughed, relaxing as they continued to chat. She had been a part of his life for so long. She wasn't his mother and never tried to be, but she had become the maternal figure he'd looked to growing up. He believed his own mother would have liked her... and approved of her for his dad now.

"Hi, Mom!" Brooke called out from the front of the house, and he was grateful to get out of his own head.

He was even happier Brooke was home. Aiden hadn't heard the door open or close but her high heels clicked on the wooden floor as she approached, and a sense of awareness washed over him.

She stepped into the kitchen, looking gorgeous in a raspberry wrap dress that hugged her breasts and accentuated the sensual curve of her waist. The hem stopped above her knees and the stilettos on her feet made her legs look a mile long.

His cock stood up and took notice, his entire body heating at the sight of her. He stared without shame as she crossed the floor to her mom.

"Here you go," Brooke said, handing her mother a grater he hadn't noticed in her hand.

"Thanks for bringing this from the gatehouse."

She smiled. "Of course. Dinner smells good."

"Thanks, honey," Lizzie said.

"Hi, Aiden." The words sounded forced but at least she wasn't ignoring him.

He inclined his head and smiled. "Brooke."

"You look pretty," Lizzie said to her daughter, stepping back to admire her overall appearance.

"Thanks!" she said to her mother.

Pretty was an understatement, Aiden thought. The mere sight of her had his mouth watering. He needed to touch her. To kiss her. To carry her upstairs, settle her in his bed, and keep her there until he had his fill. In other words, forever.

"Where are you off to?" Lizzie asked.

Without glancing his way, she replied, "I have a date."

Just like that, Aiden's hopeful mood turned to shit.

Chapter Ten

After Brooke's pronouncement, tense silence settled over the room. She shouldn't feel guilty, yet she refused to look Aiden's way. As a single woman, she was free to date whomever she wanted. It was the same thing she'd told herself while he was off traveling the world and forgetting all about their one night together.

But the way he'd spoken to her a few days ago on the porch made her think she might have been wrong. He wanted forgiveness—though he hadn't actually *apologized*—and he'd almost kissed her. He'd spoken of their night together with a heated look blazing in his eyes, a desire that matched her own.

None of it mattered. He'd also made it clear to her a long time ago that he considered sleeping with her a mistake. He'd humiliated her when he said that night meant nothing, after she'd been so blatant about her feelings for him the morning after. While she'd believed they were starting something amazing, he'd had one foot out the door.

Still, she wouldn't have purposefully mentioned the date in front of him if her mom hadn't asked about her plans.

Her mother's eyebrows popped up in surprise, probably because Brooke hadn't gone on a date in nearly a year, and she hadn't had a serious relationship since Aiden left. Despite having tried.

"Who are you going out with?" Aiden's sharp tone was accompanied by the screech of his stool being shoved back as he rose to his feet.

What the hell?

They'd agreed not to tell anyone about their short-lived romantic relationship, so she didn't expect him to react so strongly to the news in front of her mother.

"Who is it, Brooke?" he demanded.

She straightened her spine and shot him a look of annoyance. "I don't see why you care, but Fallon set me up with a man from Noah's office."

Aiden's nose wrinkled in distaste. "Someone you don't even know?"

Brooke blinked. "So?"

"I don't like it."

She smirked at him. "Good thing I don't need your approval then."

Her mother coughed but said nothing.

"Noah knows him from work? He's not good enough for you."

She rolled her eyes, crossing her arms over her chest. "Are you kidding? You don't even know the guy."

"Neither do you. And all lawyers are slimy."

Brooke tilted her chin up in challenge. "I can't wait to tell Fallon you feel that way, considering that she's married to one."

Her mom chuckled under her breath but still didn't interject. She was busy shredding carrots and *almost* acting like she wasn't listening.

"Noah is the exception. You shouldn't go out with a stranger."

Fed up with his nonsense, Brooke spun on her heel. "Bye, Mom," she said, marching out of the kitchen.

Unfortunately, he followed her into the living room. When she headed for the front door, he blocked her path. "You need to rethink meeting up with someone you don't know."

She scoffed, balling her hands into fists at her sides as she glared at him. "I didn't ask what you think, and I'm going on this date whether you like it or not. Now, get out of my way. I'm going to be late."

She also felt an urgent need to get away from Aiden because she didn't find his protective, alpha side nearly as off-putting as she should. His apparent jealousy caused butterflies to take flight in her stomach.

But wasn't that the reason she agreed to this date? The first step in putting her feelings for Aiden behind her. She didn't want her pulse to race when he was near. She didn't want to think about his hands on her body when he treated her to his heated stare. She didn't want to burn for him anymore, period, so she had to give moving on a real chance.

"Just tell me where you're going, then. So I know you'll be safe."

Fueled by frustration and a need to put him in his place, Brooke closed the distance between them and shoved a red-painted fingernail into his chest.

"I'm not telling you anything, and it's ridiculous that you would even ask. Who I date is none of your business. You lost the right to question me like this a long time ago."

Despite speaking the truth, she also knew he had always looked out for her growing up. His protective possessiveness was part of the reason she'd fallen for him in the first place.

He shoved a hand through his hair in obvious frustration. "Maybe not, but that won't stop me from worrying."

She stepped around him, and this time he didn't stop her, so she walked out the door and headed for her car.

A little while later, she stepped into the Italian restaurant Mark had chosen. He was waiting at the table when she arrived and immediately stood and pulled out her chair like a gentleman. Her lips curved upward at the courtesy.

"You look really beautiful," Mark said, his eyes flickering up and down her body but not lingering anywhere that would make her uncomfortable.

"Thank you," she said, feeling her cheeks heat in a blush.

She settled into her seat across from Mark, taking a moment to study him. He matched his photo, but instead of being clean-shaven, he had a stubbled beard that suited him, sandy blond, like his hair. Good-looking and a nice guy. Fallon wouldn't have set her up with him otherwise.

"I'm so glad you agreed to come tonight. Fallon told me about you a while ago, but she wasn't sure whether you'd accept a date with someone you didn't know."

She smiled. "Don't take it personally. I'm not really a blind date kind of girl."

"I guess I should consider myself lucky then."

Mark had an easy grin that put her at ease. She picked up her menu and flipped it open. She'd never been to this restaurant before, but it was a nice place with a romantic vibe. A small glass vase sat in the middle of the table with a tealight candle inside. The white tablecloths were crisp, and the lighting low enough to give an intimate feel.

For the next half hour, they drank wine, shared bread, and made small talk. It didn't take long for Brooke to realize he wasn't just nice, he was charming in a way that seemed effortless. Fallon had done well. Mark was a great catch.

Unfortunately, Brooke wasn't interested in a romantic way. On paper, Mark ticked all the boxes. Successful, handsome, and easy to talk to. The only thing missing was the spark.

Sitting across the table from him, Brooke hated that she kept thinking about Aiden and the butterflies in her stomach when he demanded she skip her date. It was a ridiculous high but profound in comparison to the bland feeling she got when Mark smiled and told her she was beautiful. It wasn't fair to compare the men. But that's what she'd been doing for years, and it was a pattern she needed to break.

She couldn't see Mark again, it would be leading him on, but for tonight, she did her best to keep herself engaged in the conversation throughout the meal. Her Alfredo smelled amazing, and she eagerly twirled the pasta around her fork.

She'd taken two bites before she realized that Mark was watching her.

"I love a woman with a healthy appetite," he said. "It's always so uncomfortable when I'm eating a full meal and my date is picking at a small, undressed salad."

"Have you had a lot of dates like that?"

"More than you'd think. My sister told me that she eats *before* her dates so that guys don't think she's fat."

Brooke laughed. "That seems a little over-the-top. Everyone eats. Why would a woman pretend not to?"

"That's what I say."

He cut a piece of his chicken parmesan and took a bite. "This is delicious. Would you like to try it?"

She almost said no, but it looked good, and he was already cutting her a piece, holding his fork out to her. The act felt intimate, especially when she wrapped her lips around the fork and his eyes darkened with desire.

Still, no spark on her end.

What was wrong with her?

As soon as that thought crossed her mind, her phone dinged with a text. Mumbling an apology, she pulled it out. Since Alex's second heart attack, she never ignored her phone. But the text wasn't from her mom or anyone else with bad news. It was Aiden.

Are you thinking about me while you're with him?

She froze as she read the words, then clenched her jaw. They hadn't exchanged texts in forever, and that he'd do so now, with *this* message, was utterly shocking. And infuriating. And… *welcome.*

Dammit.

Before she could come up with something, another text came through.

Do you know how crazy it makes me to think of you with someone else?

"Is everything okay?" Mark asked.

Not at all. "Yep."

She tucked her phone away and continued to eat. Trying to get back into the conversation, she asked Mark about his job. It turned out he was a contract lawyer, which he admitted was pretty boring.

She tried to feign interest, but the conversation lulled. She was the problem, not Mark. Her phone hadn't gone off again, but she'd come to the realization that she wanted Aiden to send another message.

"Excuse me. I'm going to the men's room," Mark said, placing his napkin on the table. "I'll be right back."

As soon as he was out of sight, she pulled out her phone once more, having come up with a reply to Aiden's message about how crazy it made him to think of her with someone else. She'd just send one message and refocus on Mark.

She typed out a response. *You didn't care if I dated someone else while you were gone.*

Hoping that was enough to end the conversation, she started to tuck her phone away again, but he responded quickly.

Oh yes, I did. I just convinced myself I'd done the right thing.

Hurting her had been the right thing to do? Damn him.

This time, she turned off her phone. To hell with Aiden. She was going to direct her focus where it belonged: on her date. Spark or not, Mark deserved her full attention.

Aiden did not.

Chapter Eleven

AIDEN PACED THE length of the living room, his phone in his hand. He'd sent three more texts to Brooke after confessing he'd rejected her because he'd convinced himself it was the right thing to do. No reply. No read receipt, either.

From the moment she announced she was going on a date, he'd been spiraling. Jealousy and possessiveness were new to him, no doubt because he'd never had to see the results of his breakup with Brooke. Never had to think about her with another man.

Now she was out and though he didn't think she'd go home with someone she just met, his mind ran wild with what-ifs. He might have no right to his feelings, but he owned them nevertheless.

He couldn't stay here, waiting for her to come home. He needed a distraction and decided to take a walk. Leaving the house, he strode past the gatehouse and off the property. The suburban area was full of large estates like his father's, but there was also a nature park nearby.

He walked, his steps unhurried as he winded

around the familiar path. He used to spend time here when he was younger and they'd first moved into the house. He'd still been grieving the loss of his mother, and it was tough to adjust to all the changes, including a new house. His big family could be a blessing, but at other times, a curse.

Privacy and silence were hard to come by, so he would escape. Three hundred acres of wooded area featured trails, a pond, and preserved wildlife habitats with benches throughout. It was beautiful and peaceful. Even as he worried that Brooke was having a great time with another man, walking down the path through the woods helped to calm his mind.

The sun was low in the sky, but there was still plenty of natural light allowing him to enjoy his surroundings. He didn't stay long, but the anxiety that had been overtaking him earlier had receded by the time he started the short walk home.

He still wasn't happy that Brooke was on a date, and if she'd told him where she was, he probably would have shown up there and made a scene. This way, he spent his time at the park forcing himself to remember that Brooke had been a single woman since he departed New York. She could have found someone else to love in that time, but she hadn't. He had to believe that meant he had a chance of winning her back.

His thoughts were focused as he returned to the house, and he was already halfway up the driveway before he noticed a man in a black suit standing near his car. Aiden's gut churned as he approached.

The stranger's presence on private property was alarming enough, but his shaved head, tattoos, and expressionless face told Aiden he wasn't here for a friendly chat. The man was tall and broad, bigger than Aiden. But his unnatural stillness sent a shiver down Aiden's spine. He didn't shift his weight from foot to foot or adjust his clothes. He stood in place, his arms at his sides. Not even his eyes moved.

They just stayed focused on Aiden and he braced as he approached. "Who are you?" Aiden asked, stopping farther than arm's length away. "This is private property."

"You already know what I want," the man said, his accented voice deep and commanding.

Yes, he did, but the reality still had a tight knot forming in Aiden's stomach. They'd done enough research on him to know where he was staying. He straightened to his full height and crossed his arms over his chest. "I don't appreciate being threatened."

There was a moment of tense silence as the man stared at him, but Aiden held his ground.

"It wasn't a threat, Mr. Sterling. We never start with threats. But most people appreciate a friendly warning first."

The man reached in this pocket, and Aiden stiffened, preparing for him to pull out a weapon, but it was just a pair of leather gloves. Considering the season, late summer, the move was meant to intimidate. Aiden wasn't afraid to admit it worked and his heart slammed against his chest.

"Apparently, the earlier messages might not have been clear enough," the stranger said, pulling on one glove, then the other. "So, I'll give you some clarity. If you don't kill the story, trouble will find you."

That sounded a hell of a lot like a threat to Aiden. "Who are you?" he asked again.

"Me? I'm the messenger sent to get you to see reason. If a friendly warning won't get you to act in your own self-interest, then name your price to destroy the article. You might be wealthy but everyone wants more money, no?"

"What?" Aiden hadn't anticipated being bribed, but he had his answer ready. "You can't buy me," he said. "The truth *will* come out."

The man shook his head slowly, almost mockingly. "Such a shame. I thought you were smarter than that. I suggest you think about it. *Do. The. Right. Thing.*"

Oh, he planned to, Aiden thought. They just didn't agree on what that was.

With a salute and a smile that didn't reach his eyes,

the man walked away and into the woods. Aiden watched him go, unease slithering down his spine. They knew where he lived and had obviously done a background check on him if they knew about his trust fund.

Once the man disappeared from view, Aiden went inside for a glass of his father's brandy. The house was quiet and he assumed Lizzie and his father were in the TV room on the other side of the house.

He took a healthy sip and over time, the stiff drink calmed his nerves. The stranger's threats—because that's what they were—and the attempt to bribe him weighed heavily on his mind.

He'd known that writing the article would be dangerous but once he returned home, that risk seemed far away. Even when he'd received the note telling him to kill the story, the threat didn't hold nearly as much weight as this stranger who'd made his way onto the property.

Aiden thought about calling the police, but he had no proof, no idea who the man was, and escalating the situation and potentially making it public seemed like a bad idea. But his brother, Remy, used to be NYPD and now worked as a private investigator. If anyone could help him, it would be his brother.

Except Remy and his wife, Raven, were on the other side of the world on a luxury vacation in Japan.

They'd planned for it and had been excited for a while and Aiden didn't want them to cut the trip short. Raven might throttle him if he did, he thought with a grin. Of course, she'd understand, but he refused to disrupt their vacation. With two and a half weeks until publication, he had time to wait until Remy returned.

Headlights flashed through the windows from the driveway as a car drove past the main house and toward the gatehouse. Aiden rose to his feet and strode out the back door by the kitchen, assuming that car was Brooke's. He had no plan, no idea what he'd say, but he knew he had to see her.

He reached her as she exited her car, her back to him, her concentration on locking the vehicle.

"Brooke."

She spun around, her eyes round with surprise. "Oh my God, Aiden, you scared me."

He held his hands up in an *I mean no harm* gesture, and she relaxed, her shoulders dropping as she laughed.

Her reaction had him grinning while he barely held back the urge to pull her into his arms. For just a moment, it felt like old times, when they were friends and things weren't so complicated. But as much as Aiden missed their friendship, he wanted to recapture their feelings for each other more. He wanted the relationship they could have had if he hadn't been young and stupid, and he'd chosen differently.

As the laughter faded, he gave in to the urge to touch her. Stepping closer, so only inches separated them, he grabbed her by the hips and pulled her body into his. Her delicious curves aligned with his harder edges, and he groaned.

Brooke's eyes flashed with heat as his erection pressed against her stomach.

"You're so beautiful," he said.

She splayed her hands across his chest, and tilted her head, staring into his face. He sucked in a long breath. Her flushed cheeks, glazed eyes, and plump lips beckoned to him, and he hadn't even kissed her yet.

His heart pounded as he lowered his head, ready to get a taste of her after all these years. Taking him off guard, she rose onto her toes and kissed him first.

Her soft lips met his and with a groan, he wrapped an arm around her waist and deepened their connection. His tongue slid into her mouth and as he tasted her, he found heaven. Everything he'd been looking for was right here, in his arms.

He lifted her, and she hugged him tight, wrapping her legs around his waist. He wasn't certain how long they stood making out on the driveway, but he could have gone on forever.

His dick was hard, but his focus was on kissing

her. He slid his lips to the side, trailing damp kisses down her neck and back up, nuzzling his nose into her neck.

"You smell so good," he said in a gruff voice. "I dreamed of that scent."

Without warning, she pulled her head back, breaking their connection. "Aiden. No. We shouldn't." She released her arms, then her legs, and slid down his body.

Respecting her boundaries wasn't easy, but he stepped back and waited for her to explain what was going on in her head.

When she remained silent, he met her gaze, turned on by her kiss-swollen lips and flushed cheeks. "Is it your date? It went well?" He hated the possibility yet asked in a calm, reasonable voice.

"Actually, it went very well," she said.

He stiffened and forced himself not to react or give her a reason to shut him out.

"But I'm not going to see him again."

Yes! He curled his hands into fists but kept his elated emotions in check.

She sighed. "Look, you and I have unfinished history. And it's obvious we're still... attracted to each other. But we need to work on our friendship, that's all. Me ignoring you, and you trying to sabotage my date, won't work."

An inappropriate smirk lifted his lips. "Is that what I did?"

She rolled her eyes. "Yes, you tried to mess up my night. What else would you call it?"

He really shouldn't say what he was thinking. "Staking my claim. And that kiss just proved it."

She raised her hands and lowered them fast in frustration. "Argh! You can't stake a claim on what you willingly gave away."

He folded his arms across his chest, determined to get his point across. "We are long overdue for a conversation."

She placed her hands on her hips and raised her brows. "You mean acting like an asshole about my date doesn't count as a proper conversation?" Despite being serious, her lips lifted in an amused grin.

"I get it. Now, why aren't you going to see him again?" If the date went as well as she'd said, he wanted to know the reason.

She shook her head, and let out groan, her exasperation evident. "Because he isn't you, okay? I'm still angry, I'm hurt, I need to get over you, but dammit, Aiden, it isn't easy. And then you go and kiss me—"

"Umm… I hate to point it out, but you kissed me first."

"Aiden!" Her hands flew up in more frustration.

He held in a laugh, surprised by his good mood,

but no matter what she said now, she couldn't erase that kiss from his mind.

"I need to go inside," she muttered.

He knew when to call it a night. "Okay, sleep well."

"Thank you." She turned and walked back toward the house, delicately due to her heels.

He had no doubt she'd feel better if she could stomp back and slam the door in his face. Again. She wasn't upset with him, she was angry with herself for letting down her inhibitions and walls, if just for a short time.

As she topped the few steps of the front porch, he called her name. "Brooke."

She looked over her shoulder.

"I missed you, too." She hadn't said those words, but he could read between the lines—or should he say, between her lips with that kiss. "And I want more from you than friendship."

Ignoring him, she let herself into the house and shut the door behind her.

He stood there for a moment longer, unreasonably pleased with how things between them had gone. First, she wouldn't be seeing her date again because of him. She hadn't pushed him away and she'd been all in on that kiss. And despite her frustration with the past, and the present, he'd made headway.

Either that or he was delusional. Regardless, he'd take it.

Shoving his hands into his pants pockets, he strode back to the house in a much better mood than when he'd left.

Chapter Twelve

MONDAY MORNING, BROOKE stood in the shower, hot water cascading down her body. She went through her normal routine, her hands moving on autopilot as she washed her hair and shaved her legs, her mind a million miles away. Or rather, stuck on the man living in the house across the way.

His jealousy and flirty texts, the kiss, all painted a picture. He wanted more than friendship, he'd admitted as much. Unlike him, her heart and her head were in conflict. She loved him and always had, but forgiving him came with risks. The man had traveling and journalism in his blood. He might be home now to help his family, and he might even be telling himself he wanted to stay. She didn't trust him to keep his word.

But she did believe he was going to attempt to get her to change her mind. Which meant it was going to be damned hard to resist him and keep with her plan to move on.

She rinsed the soap from her body, her hand moving over her sex, and she paused, her mind still on

Aiden. Just thinking about him had a low throbbing settle between her thighs, reminding her that her body knew *exactly* what it wanted. Who it wanted.

Ever since he'd pressed her against the wall on her front porch, a long dormant part of her had reawakened. Her response to his kiss merely confirmed it. The overwhelming desire she'd only ever felt for Aiden had returned and grew worse with each heated interaction between them.

He'd gripped her hips and the naked need in his eyes matched the way her body overheated, the kiss leaving her aching for relief. As a result, she hadn't slept well since her date. She leaned against the shower tile, closed her eyes, and lost herself in the memory of the one time she'd spent with Aiden.

His big hands settled on her breasts, his tongue tangled with hers, and his erection was long and thick as he sank deep inside her. Lost in the memories, Brooke let her hands roam, her fingers pinching one nipple while the other hand slid over her stomach and reached her clit.

She rubbed the sensitive nub in a tight circle, her legs shaking as she remembered Aiden's tense expression as he pounded into her. She recalled the squeaking of the bedframe and the sounds they made as pleasure consumed them both.

Echoes of that rapture resonated now as her climax built up inside her, need coiling tighter and tighter. Aiden had buried his face in her neck as he came, groaning her name with each thrust. The water turned lukewarm as she moved her hand lower, thrust two fingers deep inside and…

Why did she feel water high around her ankles? Removing her hands, her sex aching, her orgasm unfulfilled, she glanced down at the rising water. The moment of bliss was lost to a plumbing issue. The drain wasn't working.

She turned off the water and cursed under her breath. Whipping the shower curtain aside, she wrapped a towel around her body and stepped onto the bathmat. A glance at the sink told her there was water backing up there as well. It had been draining slowly lately, but she'd ignored the problem, hoping it wasn't a big deal. She hadn't mentioned the issue to her mom, either.

Heading to her bedroom, she dressed quickly, braiding her damp hair to get it out of her face. She grabbed her phone off the nightstand and pulled up Aiden's number. It wasn't until the phone was already ringing that she realized she could have called Alex or *anyone* else in the Sterling family to handle this situation.

Aiden answered before she could hang up and try someone that she didn't have a complicated relationship with.

"Brooke? You okay?"

She heard the panic in his voice, and she had to admit, his concern got to her. "I'm fine. There's a problem with the plumbing and the water is backed up in the bathroom."

"I'll be right there."

He hung up before she could protest. She hadn't expected him to rush over to the gatehouse. She just thought someone should know so they could call a plumber.

Or had she really wanted him here?

She wrung out the bottom of her braid some more, finishing as the doorbell rang. She walked down the short flight of stairs to meet him at the door.

"Hi," she said, as she opened the door.

"I'm glad you called." He was dressed in a suit, ready for work, yet he'd still rushed over. "Mind if I check the kitchen sink first?"

"Go ahead."

He walked past her and she stared at his back, intrigued by the way he moved in dress clothes. Used to him in more casual attire, this business side of him was sexy, too. She sighed, her body still tingling from the unfulfilled masturbation session.

"Yep. Kitchen sink is backed up, too," he said.

She glanced over his shoulder and saw a few inches of dark water in the metal basin and wrinkled her nose.

"The garbage disposal shutting off was probably a coincidence but since the water is in the bathroom and the kitchen, there must be a clog somewhere in the drainage system," Aiden said.

She was more focused on the heady scent of his cologne than the house problem. She warned herself not to sway closer to him for a sniff.

"That's bad, right?" she managed to ask.

He turned unexpectedly, and they were too close. "It's not an easy fix like resetting the disposal. I'll call someone to come look at it."

"Do you think they can fix it the same day?" she asked, hopefully.

He shrugged. "No idea. This kind of thing isn't my forte. We'll just have to see what a plumber says. I'll let you know as soon as I reach someone."

She reached out before she could overthink and placed a hand on his arm. "Thank you."

"You don't have to thank me, Brooke. I'm here for you, anytime."

His sincerity struck her in the heart and despite all her internal misgivings, a rush of affection filled her chest and warning bells went off in her head.

Sexual tension was something she was used to. She'd always desired Aiden. But this caring feeling? It had been a while since she'd experienced warm emotions toward him and the feeling reminded her that before he'd left home, he'd always been someone she could count on.

Shaken, she took a step back. "I'd better go change," she said, breaking contact. "I have to get to the office."

He nodded, his knowing gaze never leaving hers. "Go ahead and I'll let you know."

"Thanks," she said, watching as he left.

As she drove to the office, she couldn't get him off her mind. He'd looked and sounded so sincere when he told her he was there for her. It was almost as if he *wanted* her to call him whenever she needed help. *Wanted* to be there for her.

The tender feelings she'd felt in the past were officially back, just as strong as before.

Chapter Thirteen

AIDEN SPENT HIS Monday morning calling plumbers. He made five different phone calls before he found one with an opening in his schedule to come right over. Offering him double to make time had helped. That Brooke called *him* when she needed help meant something, and he wanted to come through for her.

The man had arrived before noon and now Aiden was at Sterling Investments and walking toward Brooke's office with bad news. He stopped by her open door and glanced inside.

She sat at her desk, her gaze on her laptop screen. As she read, she tapped a pen on the wooden desk surface, oblivious to his presence, giving him time to study her. She'd kicked off her shoes, revealing painted red toenails to match her fingers. A teal-colored dress fitted her curves yet was completely work appropriate. Whether she wore casual clothes or dressed for the office with a full face of makeup, she was stunning.

He knocked.

She whipped her head toward him, and for the first time, greeted him with a smile. "Hi, Aiden. Come on in."

He stepped into the office and shut the solid door behind him, appreciating the idea of a few stolen minutes alone with her. The windows provided a view of the city below them.

Though not as big as Jared's corner suite, which Aiden would take over when the baby arrived, Brooke's was spacious enough for a large desk, a leather chair, filing cabinets, as well as a couple of seats for clients in front of her desk.

The personal items spread around caught his attention. A bobblehead of Mr. Met, a team they both loved, sat on the corner of the desk. Her coffee mug had a logo from the TV show *Friends*, reminding him of how she'd binged the whole series when they were in college. Despite claiming it was cheesy, he often found himself on the couch beside her, watching the episodes while he drank a beer and she sipped wine coolers.

Tasteful art hung on the walls, abstract and colorful enough to offset the neutral off-white walls and gray carpeting. The space was comfortable for clients and perfect for Brooke.

"Did you need something?" she asked, and he realized he'd been lost in thought while she waited for him to speak.

"I met with a plumber and it's not good," he said, moving to one of the two cushioned chairs in front of her desk.

She groaned, shaking her head. "Break it to me gently."

"The problem is that a tree root broke through the drainpipe, blocking the flow. He'll need to excavate the yard in order to fix it."

"Oh, no." Brooke frowned. "How long does he think that will take?"

Thanks to some more money thrown at the man? "A couple of days," he said.

"Oh! That's not too bad!" Her shoulders relaxed, and she eased back in her seat.

He gritted his teeth at her optimism. "Actually, it is that bad. He can't start until next week." He was mid-job and even though he'd moved them up on his schedule, it would still take at least a week. More if he found problems on his current project.

"Seriously?" She lay her forehead down on the desk. "What are Mom and I going to do if we can't shower or eat at home?" she asked as she straightened in the chair.

Aiden already had her problem covered. The solution just happened to be a side benefit to him. "You and Lizzie can stay at the main house until it's fixed. I already spoke to Dad."

As expected, his father had no issue with the women moving in. In fact, Alex's eyes lit up at the prospect. Aiden had no interest in his dad's love life, but he definitely understood the man's reaction.

"Your father is the best. I'll have to thank him." Brooke bit her bottom lip, and his cock grew hard at the sight. It was amazing how pretty much anything this woman did turned him on.

He leaned forward, bracing his arms on the desk. "Don't you think I'm pretty amazing too?"

She rolled her eyes. "Yes, Aiden. You're amazing. But seriously, thank you for taking care of everything so quickly."

He preferred to focus on the first part of her statement even if he had forced her to say the words. "You're welcome."

What she didn't know was his plan for *where* in the main house she'd stay. They had plenty of rooms. All his siblings had had their own bedrooms growing up, but Aiden intended to make sure the one next to his was ready for Brooke when she brought her things over.

Would she be happy about the location? Probably not, but he resolved to change her attitude. He had one week to work on romancing her while he had her staying in the room next door.

A knock sounded on the door, saving him from further conversation that might lead to an argument about where in the house she'd sleep.

"Come in," Brooke called out.

The door opened and Jared walked in, shock registering on his face as he saw Aiden there as well. He quickly recovered, his eyes no longer wide, his mouth now shut.

"Well, this saves me from having to talk to you individually," Jared said. Stepping inside, he seated himself in the chair beside Aiden.

Brooke smiled at him. "What's going on?"

Jared glanced at Brooke, then Aiden. "I have a project for the two of you to work on together."

An excited thrill shot through him. Brooke's attitude toward him was obviously softening, but she was stubborn by nature and tended to overthink things. The only way he'd convince her to open her heart to him again was with time and persistence. Living in close quarters and working together on a project would provide both.

Brooke glanced at Jared, her gaze narrowed as she drummed her fingers on the desk, a sure sign of nerves. "What's the project?" she asked.

Jared extended his feet in front of him, leaning back in his seat. "There's a small bank about to go up for sale. Research shows that over the last three years they've suffered from a weak return of assets. The current owners are looking to cut their losses and thanks to a connection, we have an in before anyone else makes an offer."

"That's great," Brooke said. "But these deals usually take months to work out."

Jared nodded. "Exactly. I'll be out on leave, which is why I need you two to take the lead."

Aiden knew this was his opportunity to prove to Jared his faith in him was not unfounded. "Looking forward to it," he told his brother.

Brooke cleared her throat. "This doesn't necessarily call for two people. I could take lead on it myself."

Aiden held back any reaction. He wasn't surprised she'd try to ice him out in order to avoid them working closely together. For her, it obviously made her uneasy. For him, it was a golden opportunity. But he'd leave it to his brother to handle her offer. He had faith Jared would want him in on the deal so he could learn on the job.

Jared met Brooke's gaze. "I know you can handle it on your own, but we both know it's a lot for one person to take on. Besides, Aiden is still learning the business, and this is a valuable experience for him."

Just as he'd thought, Aiden mused.

"No problem." Brooke forced a smile. She wouldn't argue with the CEO.

Jared braced his hands on the arms of his chair and rose to his feet. "Great. I'll send you both an email with the details and documents attached."

Aiden stood. "Don't worry. We've got this," he assured his sibling.

Placing a hand on Aiden's shoulder, Jared said, "I know you do. And I appreciate it more than you know."

While he had Jared's attention, Aiden asked, "How's Charlie feeling?" He knew Jared couldn't wait for her to go into labor and have their baby.

"She's amazing. Nesting, or so she says. Apparently, it's a thing." He shook his head, but a grin spread wide on his face.

Brooke laughed. "Give her my best," she said to Jared.

"Will do." He walked out of the room, pulling the door closed behind him.

Aiden waited until the door clicked shut before speaking. "Worried about working closely with me?"

Brooke shook her head. "Of course not. I just didn't think it made sense to tie up two key executives while Jared is away." Her gaze slid from his as she lied.

"Me being one of the key executives?" he asked, laughing. "You are aware you know way more than me about any potential deal, and Jared's right. I need to learn."

Leaning back in her seat, she swiveled back and forth. "I suppose you're right."

"Say that again?" he teased her.

"Oh, shut up," she muttered, but he saw the half smile on her face.

Her guard was down and he decided to take advantage. He walked to the office door and locked them in, then strode around her desk, came up beside her, and swiveled her chair to face him.

She swallowed hard, her hands clenching the arms on the chair so hard her fingertips turned white. "What do you want?" she asked, a tremor in her voice.

Her heady coconut scent surrounded him as he leaned in close. "I think you know, Brookie," he said, using her old nickname.

She slid her tongue over her lower lip. Though she had time to argue, she merely stared at him, her breath coming in shorter pants.

She hadn't moved away nor had she objected, so he leaned in, placed his hands on her hips, pulling her out of her chair and into his arms. Then his mouth came down on hers.

Chapter Fourteen

BROOKE WAS STUNNED as Aiden's mouth touched hers, yet every nerve ending in her body came to life. Her heart raced, and her thoughts turned hazy as she parted her lips for him. One of his strong arms wrapped around her body and he slid the other into her hair, using the strands to tilt her head and give him better access to her mouth. Everything between them seemed right, just like when they'd been together before. Only the time and place were off.

That should have pulled her out of the moment, but she'd been fighting him and her feelings for so long. As she kissed him back, the struggle between her mind and her heart was real. But so was he, and she was so tired of the war inside her.

He lifted his head, his brown eyes dark with longing. "Don't overthink things," he said, dragging his knuckles down her cheek. "It's you, Brooke. It's always been you."

She swallowed hard. "I want to believe that." And a part of her did.

"I'm also so damned sorry." He'd slid his hands to her waist and didn't release his hold.

"What?"

"I'm sorry for not telling you about my plans to leave before we slept together, and I'm sorry for not handling it well after."

She blinked, tears forming in her eyes. It was the first time he'd apologized and, in a way, she knew he understood what he'd done wrong, and the sincerity in his voice affected her deeply. So did the sadness and remorse in his dark eyes.

He'd finally cracked open something within her, and she was ready to have the conversation that was long overdue between them.

"I needed to hear your apology," she said. "But you need to hear how you affected me."

He nodded, stiffening because he no doubt knew he wouldn't like what she had to say.

"When you made that announcement to everyone? I felt like such an immature idiot," she said, remembering the night of Fallon's party. "You said you had something to say, and I thought you were going to tell them about *us*." She paused long enough to let out a humorless chuckle even as she felt the urge to cry. But she'd done that enough over Aiden.

His eyes opened wide. "Brooke, I—"

She shook her head. "Let me finish, please." She drew a deep breath. "Looking back, I know how stupid that thought was. We weren't in a relationship;

we'd had one night together. There'd been nothing to announce. But I was full of happiness and childish hope, and I'd convinced myself of something you'd never actually said to me." She took a step back, sending her chair moving away.

"No," Aiden cut in, his voice thick with emotion. "You weren't stupid or childish. I led you on. I can see that now."

She sighed, appreciating the sentiment. "You telling us you were leaving New York was such a shock to me."

"I think I stunned the whole family," he said. "I didn't tell a soul when I applied for the job because I didn't know if I'd get it, and I was worried everyone would try and talk me out of it." He stepped away, walked around the desk, and paced across the carpet behind the chairs. "And if I'd been faced with that kind of pressure, I wasn't sure I would have been able to go through with leaving. Telling everyone after it was a done deal seemed easier."

She supposed she could understand his reasoning. "But you could have told me privately," she whispered, her throat tight.

He nodded. "I know that now." He rubbed his hand along the back of his neck. "I thought it would be easier to break the news to you at the same time as everyone else."

"Easier for who?" she asked.

"For me," he said, glancing away. "I avoided a one-on-one conversation because I couldn't face hurting you. Telling you in a group gave me distance." He met her gaze across the room. "It was the cowardly way out. And then we had that private talk anyway."

She nodded, unable to argue. The entire party had been a nightmare, her trying to act normal and happy for Fallon while her heart had been shattered. "I asked you if we could try a long-distance relationship." She refused to say what he'd told her next. She didn't think she could get those words out without crying.

He dipped his head before he walked over to her, grasping her shoulders. "I should never have told you what we had didn't mean anything. I lied, Brooke. Our night together meant everything to me."

"Then how could you do it?"

"I'd already committed to leaving, and I had to think about what was best for you," he said.

At least she was being given a glimpse into his thought process. He, like her, had been young. They'd made mistakes. She thought she knew the real reason he'd left her with no hope, but she needed both the clarity and to hear it from Aiden.

She swallowed hard. "When you texted me during my date, you said you thought you were doing what was right. You couldn't possibly have meant hurting me was the right thing to do, so explain what it meant."

"The truth? I knew I'd be in dangerous places and unsure of how often I could return home. You deserved better than to wait around for my occasional visits home. You needed to go on with your life."

She narrowed her gaze. "What I *deserved* was the chance to make my own decision, Aiden. And if you respected me at all, you would have let me choose what I wanted instead of breaking my heart!"

"You're right," he said, and pulled her into his arms. Burying his face in her neck, he whispered. "I'm so damned sorry."

"Thank you. I needed to hear that." She let out a long breath and wrapped her arms around his neck, breathing in the warm, familiar scent of his cologne, and hugging him tight.

They'd come full circle.

She'd expressed her thoughts, feelings, and pain, and he'd acknowledged them and apologized. "Where do we go from here?"

He glanced at her. "I know I want to be with you."

Her heart beat harder at his words. She couldn't hold on to anger and hurt forever, not when they'd finally hashed out the past. But there were practicalities too. And she wasn't ready to jump all in. But didn't she owe it to herself to give them a chance?

"I don't know. It's been five long years since we were together. How do we know it would even work between us?"

Aiden cupped her cheeks, and her skin tingled at the contact. "It'll work. But you're right. We do need to get to know each other again." He pressed his lips to hers but didn't linger. "Good thing we'll be living in the same house for a while."

She smirked and he let out an easy laugh, one that made her feel good about things, at least for now. "Go back to your office and work," she told him.

If she wanted to leave on time, she had a ton left to do.

He shook his head and grinned. "Yes, ma'am." He kissed her and it wasn't nearly long or deep enough.

He walked out and she watched him go, aware that having opened her mind to the possibilities of *them*, she was in trouble. Time would reveal what happened between them, and she was going to have to live with the uncertainty.

She still couldn't get it out of her mind for the rest of the day. Had she really just gone out on a date with another man in a useless attempt to forget Aiden? What a pointless experiment that had been.

A knock sounded on her office door and her heart leapt in her chest at the thought that it might be Aiden again. But when she called out for the person to come in, Jared walked into the room.

"Hey, boss."

"Hey, yourself. What are you still doing here?" he asked, looking at his watch. "It's late."

She glanced at the clock on her computer screen, noting it was a little after six p.m. "I could ask you the same thing. Don't you have a pregnant wife to get home to?"

Jared settled into the same chair Aiden had been sitting in earlier, and rubbed his eyes. "Just trying to get as much work done as possible now. I don't want to leave a mess for Aiden to deal with while I'm on leave. He's got a good head for business, but he's still green."

"He'll do fine. If he has questions, he's surrounded by solid executives who can step in."

Jared nodded. "I know. It's just hard to let go of the reins. As difficult as it is to admit, I understand how my father ran himself into the ground doing this job."

She clasped her hands together on the desk. "Which is why you have to let go more often. You don't want to end up being like your father healthwise."

He grinned. "I don't have to take it under advisement. Charlie won't let me overdo it. Especially once the baby arrives. But thanks for looking out for me."

"Of course!" Jared was like family to her. She couldn't bear to have anything happen to him.

"I saw Aiden earlier and he was in a very good mood. Much better than usual. Would you have anything to do with that shift?" Jared leaned forward. "It goes without saying I'm asking as a friend."

She flushed but figured Jared sensed more than he let on. "We came to an understanding about the past."

Jared raised an eyebrow. "Look at you, admitting you two had a past."

"Shush." She crumpled a piece of paper into a ball and tossed it at him. Of course, it landed short of hitting him.

Jared grinned. "I don't need details, but you have to know we've all had our theories about what went down."

She dipped her head. "I wanted to keep it to myself. I convinced him never to talk about it before he took off to see the world."

Jared studied her for a moment. "I'm sorry he hurt you."

"Thanks," she murmured. She didn't have to guess how he knew. She supposed her being hurt had been the obvious conclusion.

If Aiden wanted to confide in his siblings, it was long past time, but she'd have to tell Fallon first. "I have a favor. Whatever you know, or think you know, let me talk to Fallon before it becomes public?"

Jared nodded in understanding. "I had no intention of spreading gossip around the family. Having been the focus of it after I got Charlie pregnant, I know what it feels like." He shook his head. "Not fun."

"Nope."

He tilted his head to the side. "So, are you two together now?"

She shrugged. "I don't know what we are. To be honest, he scares me. The need to travel; his love of journalism in a way that may not let him stay in this country. I'm not sure what I can handle." She wasn't twenty years old and starry-eyed anymore. Thanks to Aiden, she was more wary, more jaded.

"You know what I think?" Jared asked, then continued before she could respond. "You worry too much."

Brooke pursed her lips together at the insult. "Is that supposed to be helpful?" she asked, and not in a pleasant way.

"Let me finish," he said, raising his hands up, palms out. "I'm just saying, you can get caught up in your own head and that's definitely what's happening now. Try to let things play out. See how you two do and make your decision after you live in reality a little. But while you're at it? Have some fun, Brooke. You deserve to enjoy life more."

She sighed. "You're right." She hated to admit it but she did take things too seriously and worry... a lot.

Ever since her dad passed away unexpectedly in a car accident on icy roads, that was what she did. Worry. And though she hadn't equated the two things before, Aiden leaving had been another tough loss. Everything weighed heavier after that.

She glanced at her boss and friend. "Thanks for stopping by and listening. One of the reasons I kept things quiet was because I didn't want any of you to feel caught in the middle between us."

"Don't worry about that. Ever. We all love you *and* Aiden. That's not going to change, no matter what happens."

Brooke smiled, feeling better. Talking to Jared had been helpful. She needed to live life and worry less. Whatever happened between her and Aiden? She wasn't in control of fate.

Chapter Fifteen

AFTER A LONG day at work, professionally as well as personally, Aiden left the office, his mood better than it had been in a while. Though he hadn't planned on having a conversation about the past, he and Brooke had crossed the most difficult barrier, and she was open to a relationship of some kind. After hearing her perspective on their history, he was damned lucky to get a second chance.

That he'd hurt her had been obvious. He'd known it for years. But understanding he'd taken away her autonomy by making choices for her killed him because he'd also disrespected her in the process.

She'd wanted a long-distance relationship and deep down, so had he. He should have let her make that choice and acknowledged his desires too. And he knew now that the long hours on the road, the dangerous situations, and the lonely hotel rooms would have been more bearable if he'd had her waiting for him.

As much as he wished things could be easy from here on out, he had work to do to fix things. Sex wasn't the answer, though he hoped they'd get there soon. Most importantly, he'd have to earn her trust back over time.

Leaving work, he decided to ramp up his efforts to break through her walls and he had an idea. Time might change things about a person, but there were always constants. When it came to Brooke, he knew she'd *always* had a sweet tooth. There was no way that had changed, so he decided the first step to wooing her could be surprising her with a sweet treat.

Her favorite chocolate shop was located close to the family home in the suburbs of Westchester County. He drove home from work, stopping at the shopping center where the store was located on the way.

Once inside, he knew exactly what to buy. *Caramel.*

The memory that popped into his mind had been from a long time ago. Brooke had just gotten her driver's license, and her mom had saved up to buy her a car. She'd had her license for a week and was eager to drive anywhere, so she'd agreed to do the grocery shopping for her mother.

Aiden had helped her unload the groceries. As they brought in the last bags and placed them on the kitchen counter, Brooke reached into one of the paper bags and pulled out a purple and gold bag when Lizzie wasn't looking. Brooke winked at him and strolled out of the kitchen, bag in hand, Aiden hot on her heels.

Catching up to her in the living room, Aiden plucked the bag out of her hands, eyeing the individually wrapped caramel-filled chocolates.

"Was this on the shopping list?" he asked with a smirk, holding the bag over her head when she tried to snatch it back.

She grinned. "No, but call it my shopping and delivery fee," she said, a defiant glint in her eye. "Are you going to rat me out?"

Aiden opened the bag and pulled out one of the wrapped candies before handing the bag back to her. Unwrapping the chocolate, he ignored her annoyed glare as he popped it into his mouth. "Your secret is safe with me."

Brooke loved caramel chocolates, and now, he was going to use that knowledge to his advantage. The selection of caramel options at the chocolate shop was impressive. Dark and milk chocolate. With and without nuts. Chewy or soft caramel. Some had sea salt and others didn't. He grabbed a box and filled it with basic milk-chocolate candies filled with caramel.

After paying, he stepped out of the store. It was still light out, normal for summer, and he strode across the lot toward his car. The shop was in a strip mall with other stores, and the lot had a myriad of people coming and going.

Out of an abundance of caution, Aiden glanced

around, seeking out the guy who'd paid him a visit the other night or anyone else who might be looking his way. But all the people seemed to be going about their business, not paying anyone extra attention. Aiden couldn't explain why, but he had the same unsettling feeling he'd experienced at the coffee shop with John.

He was being watched.

He expected whoever wanted him to pull the story wouldn't give up, but as Aiden hadn't seen the stranger since after his walk in the park, he'd been trying to convince himself nothing would come of the man's threats.

Shaking off the uneasy feeling that raised the little hairs on the back of his neck, he made his way across the lot toward his car, digging his keys out of his jacket pocket. He was only about halfway there when the roar of an engine caught his attention and he glanced to the right.

A car was racing toward him. His heart stopped, his breath stalled in his lungs, and his mind struggled to understand what was happening. His brain kicked in as the vehicle accelerated and he dove to the side, landing on the hard asphalt between two sedans just as the vehicle sped past, whizzing through the spot where he'd been standing.

Dammit.

He started to get to his feet, but as he pushed

against the ground, pain sliced through both hands. He winced and glanced at his bleeding palms. His less-than-graceful landing had scraped up his skin. Thanks to the adrenaline rush, he hadn't felt the pain, but he did now.

What were the chances the driver of the SUV had just been careless, in too big of a hurry? He shook his head. More likely, they were trying to shut him up for good.

TWO HOURS LATER, Aiden sat on the couch at home, waiting for Brooke to arrive. Tonight was her first night living in the main house until the plumbing at the gatehouse was fixed and he'd been looking forward to their forced proximity.

Even better, his father had texted him while the paramedic was wrapping his palms, informing Aiden that he and Lizzie were going out for dinner. Their night out was welcome. Aiden wouldn't have to answer questions about the bandages on his hands.

He didn't need the painful reminder. He'd been reliving the moment since it happened. The sound of the engine echoed in his mind and his just-in-time dive out of the way. Such a close call. His heart rate sped up in his chest.

Rising, he walked to the kitchen. His hands shook as he pulled scotch from the cabinet above the stove, where his dad stashed the good stuff, although he wasn't partaking much anymore because of his heart. Using his fingers and being careful not to drop the bottle, he poured a glass and took a long sip.

He'd tried to stay calm after the incident, to think rationally and not jump to conclusions about who had been behind the wheel, but as he took another sip of whisky, feeling it burn down his throat, he had to admit he was shaken.

He hadn't thought they'd try and kill him... until now. It didn't make sense. The article would run no matter what happened to him.

But, his death would send a message, the same as when they'd killed Ingrid. But her murder hadn't stopped him. If anything, he'd been more driven to bring the corruption to light. No matter what happened to Ingrid or to him, once the world became aware, the investigation would continue.

All he knew was that the threat to his life felt very real, and he needed to be more careful from now on. This couldn't last forever, and with luck, the article's release would put an end to the danger. There was the potential for revenge once the story ran, but whoever was after him would be too busy with avoiding arrest. The police were now involved, not that they were convinced it was anything other than a speeding driver, but they would investigate.

Before he could continue to let his thoughts spin in his head, he heard the front door open and the sound of footsteps in the hall.

He strode out of the kitchen to see Brooke walking through the entryway, her leather tote slung over one shoulder, purse over the other, dragging a suitcase behind her. She paused where she stood.

Brooke had been in this house many times over the years, hanging out with him, having sleepovers with Fallon, and for family gatherings which always included her and Lizzie.

Her hesitation now surprised him. "What's wrong?" he asked, setting his empty glass onto the foyer table.

She closed the door behind her and set her briefcase on the same table. "I just… feel weird about staying here. Like I'm intruding."

Though he understood, he didn't want her to feel uncomfortable. "Don't be silly," he said lightly.

Brooke narrowed her gaze. "Don't call me silly. It's just strange. I'm going to be *living* here. At least, temporarily."

Aiden raised his hands up in a gesture of surrender, and Brooke's annoyed expression faded away.

Instead, her eyes grew wide, and she rushed toward

him. "Oh my God. What happened?" she asked, grabbing his wrists and staring at the white bandages.

Shit. He hadn't been thinking about the bandages when he showed her his palms. "Nothing to worry about. I just have to leave them wrapped overnight to prevent infection," he said, avoiding what she was really asking.

"But... what *happened?*" A concerned look settled on her face, and despite the seriousness of the situation, he appreciated her worry.

A couple of weeks ago, he'd been sure she hated him, so he was grateful for any sign of her caring. He'd thought about what to tell her when she asked, had even considered lying, but he couldn't do it. They wouldn't make progress together if he withheld information now. He just didn't want her to freak out when she heard.

"I was almost run down in a shopping center parking lot earlier. I dove out of the way and did a number on my palms."

"Run down?" she asked, her voice rising. She gripped his wrists tighter and the blood rushed from her face, leaving her pale. "I can't believe this. People are in too big a hurry sometimes. I mean, if they were going so fast they almost hit you..." She trailed off, studying his face. "Wait a minute. You don't think someone was trying to hit you on purpose, do you?"

He didn't know what she saw in his expression, but she knew how to read him.

He shrugged. "To be honest, I don't know what to think. I was working on a story before I came home and there was definitely danger involved," he hedged, holding back information. There was no reason to scare her further with the details of his article and the other incidents. She'd panic if she knew someone had actually threatened him.

And maybe he didn't want to admit the truth out loud.

"What did the police say?" she asked, her voice trembling.

He wished he had more information there. "They retrieved security footage from one of the stores nearby and did get a plate number. I just have a feeling they won't come up with anything." These people were too smart.

"Well, we'll just have to wait and see."

He liked how she said *we* when it came to his situation.

"What were you doing at the shopping center, anyway?" she asked, releasing his wrists.

Aiden's eyes shifted to the coffee table in front of the couch, where the plastic bag from the chocolate shop was sitting. "I went to buy you something."

Brooke turned and saw the bag with the logo from

the chocolate shop printed on the side. She walked over and picked up the bag. Reaching inside, she pulled out the now half-smashed box of chocolates.

"I landed on it," he explained.

"Caramels?" she asked, reading the label on the box. "You got me chocolate caramels?" Her voice was soft, her eyes warm with appreciation.

"They're your favorites, right?"

Brooke smiled. "If I remember correctly, *you* like them too." She opened the box and picked up one of the small, rose-shaped chocolates, popping it into her mouth and moaning at the taste.

The sound reminded him of her noises when they made love and Aiden's dick hardened with the memory.

"Would you like one?" she asked, holding out the box to him.

He wanted something much sweeter than chocolate. He wanted the delicious satisfaction of being with Brooke. At the thought, desire pumped through his veins.

He nodded anyway. "I'd love one. But... I can't grab it with my wrapped hands." He lied, and he was pretty sure she knew that, something she confirmed with a shake of her head and an amused smirk. "Feed me."

She lifted another chocolate from the box and held

it up to his mouth.

Holding her gaze, he parted his lips, and as she slid the chocolate in he swiped his tongue over her fingers. Her breath hitched, and she leaned close. Only inches separated them, the warmth of her body and her light coconut scent overwhelming him.

Swallowing the chocolate, he dipped his head and pressed his lips to hers in a kiss that turned his desire into something deeper, a need to be inside her with a desperation he'd never felt before.

Breaking their connection, he looked deep into her eyes. "Come to my bed, Brooke."

Chapter Sixteen

BROOKE HAD ALWAYS been an overthinker, as Jared pointed out to her. Someone slow to make decisions, always considering every angle, trying to predict the outcome before committing to a course of action. In business, it had proven to be a useful trait.

In her personal life, not so much.

So, as Aiden waited for her to decide if she'd join him in bed, she remembered Jared's advice.

Have some fun, Brooke.

This probably wasn't what he had in mind, but she decided to take his words to heart. She was tired of worrying about what would happen, of letting the hurt from the past hold her back in the present. She'd shut off her brain and go with what her heart and body wanted.

Shaking, she nodded, and Aiden wrapped an arm around her waist, leading her to his room.

No sooner had they entered the bedroom than he kicked the door closed and pulled her into his arms, the bandages on his hands not slowing him down. If he were in pain, he didn't show it. Instead, he cupped her face in his palms, and his mouth came down on hers. His tongue forced its way through her barely parted lips and he kissed her. She willingly went along for the ride.

Reaching down, he pulled up her black dress and she helped him maneuver it over her head. He might not worry about his palms but she clearly did.

Aiden stepped back and admired her, his eyes gleaming as he took in her black lace bra and matching panties. She hadn't dressed with him in mind but she was glad now that she loved sexy underwear.

"Fuck, Brooke. Take your bra off, sweetheart. That, I can't do."

She nodded and reached behind her to unhook the clasps, then let the garment slide to the floor. He'd used the time to take off his shirt and unbutton his pants.

"Panties next," he said, his gaze steady on her body.

She liked how he ordered her around in the bedroom. Hooking her thumbs into the sides of her underwear, she wriggled them down her legs, aware that he was removing his slacks and boxer briefs at the same time. She kicked them aside and stood naked before him.

"You're gorgeous," he said in a gruff voice.

Her gaze slid to his long, thick erection and she swallowed a moan.

He stepped toward her, grasping her hips and easing her back until her knees hit the edge of the mattress and she fell onto the bed.

He followed, his body coming over hers. "Do you know how often I've wanted you in bed with me? Any bed?" he asked, his voice rough with desire. "I thought about it every night we were apart."

"As much as I did?" she asked.

He braced himself over her, rolling his hips forward until his erection glided over her clit. She let out a moan and he grinned, then bent his head and swirled his tongue around one hard nipple.

Arching her back, she cried out, feeling the pulsing need deep in her sex. She grabbed his hair, holding him in place. He bit down lightly on her nipple, then began to lavish her breasts with attention, licking, sucking, nibbling, back and forth between each.

She'd never come from breast play alone, but for the first time, she thought she could. Of course, it would be this man to bring her to the edge.

"God, Aiden." She wrapped her legs around his waist. "I missed you."

He lifted his head. "I never stopped missing you," he said, his words sounding guttural and raw.

He rubbed his cock against her clit again, back and forth while he sensually tortured her breasts with his mouth. Suddenly, she began to shake, an orgasming slamming into her with such force, she could do nothing more than rock her hips into his and take her pleasure.

Waves of sensual bliss ruled, white lights flashing behind her closed eyes. When gratification subsided, she settled against the mattress and realized Aiden's fingers had trailed down her sides, his gaze on hers.

"I can't believe you watched me," she said, a heated flush rising to her cheeks.

He grinned the sexy smile she adored. "Once you started to come, I couldn't *not* watch." He lifted his hips and lined himself up at her entrance, then paused, cursing under his breath.

"What's wrong?" she asked.

"Condoms are in the bathroom. Be right back." He rolled out of bed.

Watching him walk away, his firm, toned ass a pleasure to view, she mulled over the idea of him traveling with condoms on him... until she heard the sound of paper being ripped open, before he returned, a strip of packets in hand.

"New box?" she asked, hating the hope in her tone. She wouldn't ask his history. Though there hadn't been many men, she hadn't been celibate, and she wasn't a hypocrite. She just didn't want to think about either of them with other people.

"Only for you, sweetheart." He crawled back onto

the bed, ripped off one condom, and lay back. He held up his hands, the gauze in sad shape but still covering his palms. "Care to do the honors?"

Smiling, she took the packet and ripped it open, then held his cock in her hand. The silky hard length felt so good in her palm. She rolled the rubber down his shaft and he groaned as she covered him.

"I'm hoping one day we won't need these," he said.

She was on birth control, and she would trust him if he told her he was tested and fine, but she wasn't ready for that kind of intimacy. Though she had a hunch after this time together she was going to be in over her head with Aiden anyway, that wasn't a step she was ready for.

When she didn't reply, he sat up and settled over her, his cock poised at her entrance. Then, raising his hips, he buried himself to the hilt. Her heart raced as she felt him inside her again. Memories of the past mixed with the present, melding into the amazing feeling of their joined bodies.

"Wrap your legs around me," he said.

She did as he asked, locking her ankles around his back, her pelvis tipping upward, giving him deeper access. Her inner walls clenched around him, pleasure filling her.

As he began to pump in and out, slowly at first,

then picking up speed, her pulse pounded in time to his thrusts. Her heart raced, her heels digging into his lower back. He held nothing back, taking her roughly while she moaned and peppered kisses along his neck and shoulder, needing her own connection to him.

Aiden whispered filthy, erotic words in her ear about how hot and wet she was, how good it felt to be inside of her. His breath warmed her neck, sending a shiver down her spine. Pressure and pleasure built inside her, her thoughts hazy and her muscles quivering, an out-of-body experience taking her higher.

She was nearing her peak when Aiden suddenly pulled out. "Aiden, what are you doing? Why are you stopping?" She reached for him as his weight lifted off her.

Before she could protest more, his big hands grabbed her hips and turned her to the side. Lifting one of her legs over his hips, he slammed back inside her, groaning as they came together once more. He slid one hand between them, his finger finding her clit. He rubbed in a tight circle, continuing his rough thrusts inside her.

"Oh, God!" she cried out, gasping as he took her hard. "Yes. *Yes!*" Her release peaked and she dangled at the edge, ready to free-fall into a sea of pleasure.

"Say my name," he demanded. "Who is going to make you come?" he asked, his brown eyes staring into hers. He pinched her clit between his fingers.

"Aiden!" Pleasure flew through her and she cried out, her body jerking against him.

He held her in place as she rode out her orgasm. "Fuck, Brooke. I can feel you coming," he groaned, as she heard his own climax take hold. His hips jerked once, then twice, before he stiffened and came hard.

Sweaty and limp, she gasped when he pulled out. She was totally sated and already her mind reentered panic mode. Their time together was better than her memories, more than she'd ever imagined they could be, which meant she was vulnerable to him all over again.

He slid off her and rose from the bed, walked back to the bathroom, a faint glow now lighting the room. He returned a few minutes later with a damp washcloth.

She held out a hand for the small towel but he shook his head. "Let me take care of you," he said in a gruff voice. "I've wasted so much time without you, and I... I just need to take care of you tonight."

More intimacy, she thought, her heart skipping a beat. She wanted to fight him, but she didn't have the strength, nor did she really have the desire. This one night, she could give in.

"Are your hands okay?" she asked, speaking of his injury.

He nodded. "I took off the bandages. I'll just have to be careful until I can rewrap them in the morning."

Accepting his answer, she rolled to her back and spread her legs, allowing him to clean her up before he tossed the washcloth to the floor.

To her surprise, his aftercare hadn't been awkward and when he slid in beside her and pulled up the covers, she didn't complain or suggest she return to her room. Her brain was fully functioning and what she'd learned when she came home earlier slammed back into her. He could have been killed tonight.

She had the definite sense he knew more than he was telling her about whether it had been a deliberate move or an accident. He hadn't lied but he had protected her from the knowledge he held back. For now, she was okay with that. She had enough fear in hearing about the incident and she couldn't handle losing him. Not when they were tentatively making their way back to each other.

So she was content to stay in his bed, let him wrap his big body around hers, and fall asleep in his arms. Talking about *them* could wait until morning.

Chapter Seventeen

BROOKE WOKE UP and knew immediately she wasn't in her own bed. She'd slept well, which surprised her, considering everything weighing on her mind. She wasn't one to easily push away things that bothered her but last night, she had. Probably because she'd slept with Aiden, and despite the past, being with him made her feel safe.

Memories of the night before came rushing back and she could admit no one ever made her feel as good and as wanted as Aiden. Sex after he'd left had been perfunctory and unsatisfying. In fact, she'd only had two partners she allowed that close, and she'd ended things quickly afterward.

Turning from facing the wall, she hoped to see Aiden still asleep beside her. His side of the bed was empty. She didn't panic, knowing she was in both his room and house. He couldn't have gone far.

But did he have regrets? Was she once again reading more into one night than he was? She sat up in bed, echoes of past humiliation reverberating inside her. The best thing she could do was go next door to her bedroom and meet up with him downstairs, fully dressed, makeup on, armor in place.

She rose from the bed just as the bedroom door opened. Realizing she was naked, she grabbed the closest piece of clothing she could find and held Aiden's shirt against the front of her body for protection.

Aiden strode into the room, tray of food in hand. His gaze took her in and he shut the door behind him with his body. "Sorry. But nobody's out there. Our parents are downstairs, but I think it's a good idea to keep that locked for now." He put the tray on the table next to the door and pushed in the button on the doorknob.

Without meeting his gaze, she pulled on his T-shirt, grateful when it fell to her upper thighs.

He carried the food to the desk in the corner of his room and set down the tray. "Breakfast is served."

She stepped over and eyed the two plates of scrambled eggs and whole wheat toast. "You cook?" she asked, surprised, though she didn't know why. There wasn't much she knew about him now.

He shook his head. "Hell, no. Your mom did. It's the same thing she made for my father, but his were egg whites."

Brooke managed a laugh. Alex wouldn't be happy with that. "Did you tell them about…" She trailed off, which was ridiculous. She was an adult.

He shook his head. "I thought it was best to keep that quiet for now. Until we both decided what happens next."

It was on the tip of her tongue to ask him what *he* wanted to happen, but since she didn't know how she felt, she wasn't ready to hear the answer. Last night hadn't fixed the problems between them, but it had knocked down her walls even more.

He handed her a cup of coffee, and she took a sip, surprised and pleased to find he'd made it just the way she liked it, with lots of sugar. He pulled out the chair at his desk and gestured for her to sit.

Once she'd settled there, he sat on the edge of the bed while they ate. She nibbled on a piece of toast, taking in all that was Aiden. In a pair of gray sweatpants, his bare chest on display, she couldn't help but admire his lean muscles. Though not a six-pack, his abs were tight, and his chest was broad with a light sprinkling of hair.

She remembered the way his sculpted muscles felt under her fingers, and her nipples turned hard as she imagined setting her plate aside and spending the morning exploring his body in the light of day.

Her gaze settled on his right shoulder, and she noticed the dark ink for the first time. "When did you get a tattoo?" she asked, taking in the compass pointing north. Though she thought hard, she couldn't figure out its meaning.

Aiden grinned and took a bite of his toast before answering. "I got that last year in Amsterdam. I found a little tattoo shop near the hostel where I was staying and I liked the look of the sketches in the window."

"Why a compass?" she asked. "Does it represent your travels?"

He held her gaze. "No. The compass facing north is about you, Brooke. You're my North Star," he said in a gruff voice.

She swallowed hard. "Even after everything, you permanently marked yourself for me?"

He took her hand. "I always knew I'd come back to you eventually. Not that I was sure you'd still be here for me, but it signified my hope."

Her heart swelled at all of it. The tattoo for her, the emotions behind it. "Aiden—"

He shook his head. "You asked, I answered. No need to get too deep right now."

She nodded and took a beat to regain her composure, then asked, "Were you in Amsterdam for work?" She changed the subject but she'd never forget the compass or its meaning.

Aiden shook his head. "No. That was a vacation."

Brooke finished off her eggs, thinking about all the experiences Aiden had over the years, how many things he'd done and seen that she didn't know about.

The truth hurt but the past had happened, and she was coming to terms with things. It helped to learn how he'd never forgotten her while he was gone.

As for his travels, though not having a home base didn't appeal to her, she was glad he'd had the chance to see the world. "You know, I wouldn't have tried to stop you from going," she said in a soft voice. She'd never have asked him to stay home. She'd just wanted him in her life.

Adien set aside his empty plate and leaned over with his elbows on his knees. Looking at her with sadness in his eyes, he nodded. "Yeah, Brooke. I know that."

She sighed and pushed away her own food. There wasn't much left and her appetite was suddenly gone.

"I have so many regrets. I don't know that if we'd tried the long-distance thing it would have worked. But I didn't even try, and that's on me."

She nodded. Staring at his serious expression, she decided it was time to be a little brave herself. "Did you know I had feelings for you long before that night we spent together?"

He opened then closed his mouth. "I didn't know. I just thought we were good friends."

She let out a laugh. "Yeah, of course you did." Leaning back in the chair, she let her mind drift to the past. "I was about seventeen when I first realized how

I felt about you. You were dating Mazie Callahan at the time, do you remember?"

"Sure. We dated for, like, two months before she moved on to a guy with a motorcycle. Apparently, he was more of a *badass.*"

Brooke chuckled as he rolled his eyes, but she grew serious again. "I didn't say anything, and maybe I should have. But our relationship wasn't like that, and I couldn't see telling you my feelings, so I kept my mouth shut. Still, I wanted you for so long, I already had those girlish dreams of happily ever after before we slept together."

He raised his head and met her gaze. "I had no idea."

"I know. I guess the point is, maybe I put hopes on you that weren't fair. When you said you didn't want to be together, you crushed my dreams, but they were *my* dreams. Not yours."

He raised an eyebrow.

"I know. It's a surprise to me, too." The words came as a shock to her, too, but they'd spawned from an unconscious part of her that just maybe was accepting some responsibility for the debacle that had happened.

He reached out and clasped her hand. "Looking back, it really does feel like I could have done better, no matter how much I didn't realize about your feelings."

She nodded. "That's true. But let me accept some of the fault. You didn't lead me on. I assumed things were more than they were."

He groaned. "You weren't. I felt everything for you. I just needed to leave."

She swallowed hard and asked the question that had been gnawing at her for years. "Why, Aiden? Why did you need to leave so badly?"

Chapter Eighteen

WHY HAD AIDEN felt the need to leave? He'd had a job most graduating seniors would kill for, a family he loved and who loved him back. Brooke had been his best friend at the time he sent out the résumés. He'd always loved the news. Loved journalism and chose that as his second major. But he'd lived in New York, could have taken an apartment in the city, and applied for news media jobs at home.

He'd already revealed the other reason he'd wanted to leave to his father. If he was going to reach for a future with Brooke, he needed to tell her the truth.

"Given your friendship with Fallon, I'm sure you know the details of how my mother died." He glanced at Brooke, who nodded, but the crinkles around her eyes told him she didn't understand the correlation. But she would.

He drew a deep breath and went on. "That night, Dad was away on business. Remy was supposed to have dinner with Mom, but he had a shot with a girl he liked, so he canceled. Mom stayed home. Fallon was upstairs asleep and I was away at summer camp when *it* happened." There was no reason to rehash the murder, not out loud and not in his head.

"Oh, Aiden. The story is so tragic. Alex is such a good man and the whole idea of an angry client..." She shook her head, obviously choosing not to speak the horrors out loud, either. "But what does that have to do with your need to travel?"

He dipped his head. "Guilt."

"What?" She reached out, touching his shoulder, and he glanced at her. "Why would you feel guilty?"

"Because if I was home... if I'd been there..." He shook his head. "And because I wasn't, she was killed. Once I understood what had happened, as I got older, the idea of getting away from New York and the memories held more and more appeal."

Unfortunately, he'd learned he couldn't run from his problems and pain.

"Aiden." Her voice sounded determined, not soft. "You were twelve years old. What could you have done against a man hopped up on drugs and determined to take revenge? Even if you were home, it would have meant your family lost two members, not just one." She clearly needed him to see the situation from her eyes.

And he did. Finally. After he'd hurt her, after he'd left his family, and after he'd been away for so long, he'd returned home and realized the same guilt had followed him around the globe.

"You're right. I see that now. Dad and I had a long talk about it when I came home."

Her gaze softened. "I'm so glad you were able to open up to him. What did Alex say?" she asked, leaning forward, listening to every word he said.

He shifted on the corner of the bed. "He said there wasn't anything any of us kids could have done to prevent the tragedy. Remy felt guilty for canceling plans with Mom, and I couldn't handle being away, but it's like you said. Maybe we would have been killed, too. Nothing can or could have altered what happened."

She rose to her feet, stepped across the carpet, and walked to him, wrapping her arms around his neck. "I'm so glad you told me."

He returned the hug, holding her tight and breathing in her warm scent. "It feels good to get it out."

"Purging toxic feelings is healthy." She shook her head. "I guess we got deep after all."

He managed a smile. "I think we were overdue." Releasing her, he leaned back. "It's all made me realize I want to look forward. The future is waiting." He didn't know what kind of future Brooke imagined for herself, but he hoped he'd be part of it.

She bit her bottom lip, a million emotions in her expressive eyes. "And what kind of future do you want?" she asked.

He'd learned a lot of lessons with her and knew the right answer. "We should date," he said, even though he was miles beyond that in his mind.

He'd known her for so long and loved her for years. His feelings for her endured even when he'd forced himself to stay away. He had no doubt what he wanted from her. But he was well aware she wasn't ready.

Relief crossed her face and she blew out a long breath. "Oh. Good. I mean, I wasn't sure what you were thinking…"

Aiden squeezed her hands, ignoring the ache in his palms from yesterday's injury. "Let me clear things up for you. I want you, Brooke. Not just in bed, but in my life. I want dates and flirty texts. I want to eat dinner with you and talk about our day, and I want to make your coffee just the way you like it in the morning and watch you smile while you drink it with messy hair and sleepy eyes."

Brooke's hand went to her head, running her finger through her hair, and Aiden chuckled.

"I want that too," she said. "But we don't know the adults we've become, so that dating time? I think it's important. And I need to know you've been home for a while and aren't going to leave again."

Her words were fair but hit hard. Knowing how

badly he'd hurt her, telling her to trust him wouldn't be enough. He had to prove to her that he deserved her.

"I understand," he said, his thumb tracing the curve of her cheek. "All I ask for is a chance."

She smiled, one that was genuine, with no hesitation. "I think I can give you that." Rising to her tiptoes, she pressed a kiss to his lips. "Don't forget to wrap your hands," she reminded him.

Then, gathering her clothes, she left the room, and he let her go without protest. He'd gotten more than he'd hoped for from Brooke last night and this morning. They had time. He showered, going through his morning routine, his thoughts lingering on Brooke. He'd never fully forgive himself for hurting her, but he wouldn't stop trying until the past stayed where it belonged and all she could see was the future.

As he stepped out of the shower, he heard his cell phone ringing and strode into the bedroom. Finding his pants on the floor at the foot of the bed, he fished the phone out of his pocket just before it went to voicemail.

"Hello?" he said, holding a towel around his waist with one hand the putting the call on speakerphone with the other.

"Hello, is this Mr. Aiden Sterling?"

The man's voice was gruff but somehow familiar.

"Yes, this is Aiden."

"This is Detective Hardwell. I took your statement yesterday." Which explained the familiarity. "I'm calling to give you an update. We've run the license plate on the SUV that nearly hit you. I'm afraid it's registered to a different vehicle. We tracked it down and determined the plate was stolen."

Shit. Though he'd expected as much, he'd hoped for a lead. Instead, it was a dead end. "What does this mean?" he asked.

"I'm afraid it means that we don't know who was driving the SUV. We tried to locate some usable CCTV footage from the area but nothing gave us a viable lead. Unless more evidence is found…"

He didn't need to finish that sentence. It had only been twelve hours, and the police had already assumed they wouldn't find any evidence of who'd been driving. The person that tried to kill him was going to get away with the attempt.

They might even try again.

Chapter Nineteen

RIGHT AFTER WORK, Brooke met Amy at yoga. She'd reached the Savasana portion, and she lay on her back, drawing in a deep breath. Beside her, Amy closed her eyes, and they both inhaled and exhaled slowly. Brooke tried to concentrate on the end of class, but she couldn't help obsessing over Aiden.

Ever since agreeing to date him, she and Aiden had gotten along well. He brought coffee to her at the office, smiling as he handed her the cup. During dinner at the house, he played footsies with her, their parents none the wiser. They'd had a quiet sort of fun during the work week, and she felt a smile curl her lips, then mentally gave herself a reprimand. Concentrating during this part of class was important.

She focused on being mindful and in the moment. She kept her breathing deep and even, her attention anchored on the sensation of taking in each cleansing breath and exhaling long and slow. When class ended, they rolled up their yoga mats and cleaned up their spaces.

Once they had their cold drinks in hand, they headed to the seating area. They paused by two women who were cleaning up and leaving their table and claimed the now empty seats.

"I saw you grinning during Savasana," Amy said, nudging Brooke's foot. "Does that mean you've slept with your boss?" she asked with a smirk only a girlfriend could manage.

Brooke had just taken a sip of her shake and nearly choked on the liquid. Hand on her chest, she swallowed and looked around.

No one was nearby, so she didn't think anyone overheard Amy, but she narrowed her eyes at her friend. "Could you be a little more discreet?"

"Sorry, but I had to ask." Amy fluttered her eyelashes, all innocent looking.

Brooke rolled her eyes at her friend. She and Amy texted a couple of times a week, so the other woman was well-versed in what was going on between Brooke and Aiden. Amy also knew, despite the date with Mark, Brooke had been weakening toward him.

"Can we say yes, I did, and leave it at that?" Brooked asked.

Amy pursed her lips and shook her head. "As if I'd settle for that after all these years. So how are things between you two now?"

"We… agreed to try dating."

Amy's eyebrows rose high. "Well, that's progress." She took a sip of her shake and met Brooke's gaze.

"I'm really proud of you. I know it can't be easy to let him in again, but you've loved him forever. I'm so glad you aren't slamming that door shut tight."

Brooke was glad too. She didn't know what the future held, but at least now she could admit that maybe there was one.

They sipped their drinks in silence, Brooke's thoughts going to her night with Aiden. It had been everything she'd hoped for and yet she couldn't deny the anxiety still plaguing her.

"What's wrong?" Amy asked.

Brooked wrapped one hand around the shake and immediately released her fingers. Too cold to use as a prop for her nerves. She met her friend's steady gaze. "I just don't want to be heartbroken again," she admitted, her voice a whisper.

Amy nodded in understanding. "Of course you don't. But what if that *doesn't* happen? What if you give Aiden another chance and you wind up getting everything you ever wanted?"

That was the real question, wasn't it?

Chapter Twenty

BROOKE SAT AT a café near the office, waiting for company. At her invitation, Fallon had agreed to come into the city for lunch. Noah had taken the day off to work from home, so he was going to take care of the baby.

It was time Brooke leveled with her best friend.

Fallon arrived ten minutes late, rushing into the restaurant, a harried look on her face. She wore one of her staple long, pleated skirts and a top that fell a drop below the waist. Brooke understood her friend's desire to cover her still swollen belly, but Fallon would be back to her cropped tops in no time. Or not. She looked amazing no matter what she wore.

Brooke waved and her friend walked over to the table, taking the seat across from her. "I'm so sorry. I missed the train I planned on taking because it took me forever to leave Gabbi and—"

Reaching across the table, she clasped Fallon's hand. "I'm sorry I asked you to come into the city. I should have visited you after work." She released her grip, wishing she'd thought more about Fallon before asking her to come.

"No! I wanted to see you. Don't forget I'm going back to work at the gallery after my three months are up. I need to get used to leaving Gabbi."

Fallon co-owned the art gallery with Clara Morganville, an older woman who'd taken Fallon under her wing. Also a talented artist, Fallon worked from home on her pop art paintings and sold them for a hefty sum. But she'd taken three months off from any kind of work to bond with her daughter and spend time with the twins.

"Well, I appreciate it." Brooke shook her napkin onto her lap and Fallon did the same. "How is the little munchkin?"

Fallon let out a long moan. "Exhausting. But also exhilarating. I won't lie though. I can't wait until she sleeps through the night."

Before Brooke could reply, a server walked over to their table, a young woman with pink tips at the ends of her hair, and smiled. "Can I get either of you something to drink?"

"Just ice water for me," Fallon said.

"A club soda with lime, please." Brooke loved a bubbly drink.

"You've got it," the woman said. "I'll be right back."

A short time later, Fallon and Brooke were each eating a salad for lunch and biting into pieces of the best French bread they'd ever tasted.

While eating, they caught up on things with the family, Fallon's baby time, Brooke's work… and then Fallon changed the subject. "Can I ask what happened with Mark?"

Despite inviting Fallon for just this reason, Brooke inwardly cringed.

"Mark told Noah he had a nice night with you, but he got the sense you weren't interested in him and he hasn't called you since." Fallon looked to Brooke for answers.

She patted her mouth with the napkin and faced her friend. "Explaining that is part of why I asked you to meet me today. I need to talk to you." Nerves fluttered in her stomach.

The last thing she wanted to do was lose her best friend because she'd kept her relationship with Fallon's brother a secret.

Fallon leaned forward in her seat. "What's going on?"

Brooke swallowed hard. "Remember you asked me if I was interested in anyone?"

Fallon nodded. "So there *is* someone?"

Brooke bit down on the side of her cheek and gathered her courage. "There's always been someone. Again, do you remember asking me in college if there was anything going on between me and Aiden?"

"I knew it!" Fallon slammed a hand on the table. The drinks shook and she cringed.

Knowing Fallon had questions, Brooke said, "Go ahead and ask."

"For starters, why didn't you tell me the truth when I asked way back when?" Fallon's tone was filled with hurt and it broke Brooke's heart.

"At the time, there wasn't anything to tell. I had feelings for him, but I didn't know if they were reciprocated. It felt awkward to tell you I liked your brother."

Fallon nodded, seeming to accept that answer. "Okay, when did you two get together and why did you stop talking for years? Because it was beyond obvious things changed between the two of you. And you avoided talking about or even looking at him. We all noticed."

Brooke took a sip of her drink before replying. No matter how many times she replayed the past, talking about it wasn't easy. "Aiden and I got together the night before your birthday party. The next night, he announced he'd taken that journalist job traveling abroad." Answering the basics was easy. Going over what came next would be more difficult.

Fallon's eyes narrowed, and Brooke could almost see her working out the situation in her mind.

"I really don't want personal details that involve

my brother, but assuming you two were *together* that night…" Fallon made quotation marks in the air with her fingers. "Then you must have already known he was leaving?" More hurt laced her tone, no doubt because Fallon thought Brooke had hidden that information from her, too.

Letting out a deep sigh, Brooke shook her head. "I had no idea." And she proceeded to explain the details, doing her best not to paint Aiden in a horrible light. The same light Brooke had seen him in for five years.

"So let me get this straight," Fallon said. "You slept with him, and he informed you he was leaving in front of the entire family?" Fallon asked, sounding horrified.

"Can I get you ladies anything?" the server asked, walking up to the table and surprising them both.

"No, thank you," Brooke said. She and Fallon needed to finish this conversation. She pushed her plate aside and clasped her hands together on the table. "How Aiden handled the situation was wrong, but I shouldn't have painted happily ever after and rainbows in my mind, either."

Fallon shook her head, then rubbed her temples with her fingertips. "I'm going to kill him."

Brooke's stomach twisted in a panic. "And that's why I never told you what happened between us. He's your brother and I never wanted to put you in the middle or make you feel like you had to choose between us."

"But—"

"No." Brooke leaned forward in her chair. "I don't want you in the middle now, either. Aiden and I have finally begun to work through the past. You getting angry at him won't help the situation. It will only put you at odds with your brother. So please, promise me you'll stay out of it?"

Fallon pouted, pursing her lips. "Well, I reserve the right to give him a brotherly smack. How's that?"

Brooke chuckled. "Fine." She supposed it was the best she could hope for. Then she turned things more personal. "Are you upset with me? For not telling you?"

With a sigh, Fallon shook her head. "I'm hurt that you went through that kind of heartbreak alone and didn't share your pain with me. I'd have been there for you, you know."

"I do," Brooke whispered. "Part of me was utterly humiliated. I didn't even tell my mom. But when it came to you, I just couldn't put you in a situation where you felt you had to choose a side."

Fallon opened her mouth to speak, but Brooke beat her to it. "And before you yell at Aiden for not telling you either, I asked him to keep it between us for the same reason. I didn't want anyone in the family to feel pulled one way or the other."

"I understand. So where do things stand now?" Fallon asked.

At least Brooke had good news to share. "We agreed to date and see how things go."

Fallon's lips curved upward in a big smile. "That's great news!"

Brooke nodded, though she was still wary. "I hope we can make things work, but you know your brother. Travel seems to be in his blood." Though he did admit he'd come to terms with the main reason he'd left home. Escaping pain that had followed him anyway. So maybe he was home to stay.

Fallon drummed her fingers on the table. "Aiden seems different now. When he used to visit, he was antsy. I could always sense he had one foot here and another in whatever country his latest story was in. Now, I see a more settled version of my brother." She paused, even her finger tapping stopped. "I think that's because of you."

"Time will tell." Brooke refused to jump to conclusions or assumptions. She'd learned that lesson the hard way.

"Well, I'm sure living under the same roof gives you quality time together."

Brooke merely hummed, not answering. She didn't

want to discuss her sex life with Aiden's sister. No matter how close they were. Besides, it was more like her lack of one.

Despite having slept together last Saturday, Brooke refused to sneak into his room at night or let him join her in her bed. She didn't know what either parent suspected, but Brooke had too much respect for Alex Sterling and her own mother to do it again.

"I think it's time for me to look for my own place." The words surprised her, but Brooke was ready. And so, she sensed, was her mom.

Her mother had survived her dad's death all those years ago and she was no longer alone. Though she lived in the gatehouse, she was dating Alex and that wasn't about to change. Brooke could move out without guilt.

Fallon nodded. "I love that for you!"

The more Brooke thought about the prospect of living on her own and decorating her own space, the more excited she got.

Chapter Twenty-One

LIVING NEXT TO Brooke and not being *with* her was torture, but Aiden understood her concerns about their parents. They needed to find someplace to be alone… or his dad and Lizzie needed to go out again. He felt like a teenager looking for a place to make out.

Friday morning, he walked to Brooke's office, a small bag in his hand. The door was open but her head was down. Before knocking, he stared, taking in her beauty. In a green sleeveless top that made her eyes pop, she was focused on the papers on her desk.

His gaze slid to her chest where the V-neck dipped low enough to show the barest hint of cleavage. He remembered how he'd used his mouth on her taut nipples last weekend, and had to collect himself, breathing deep and instructing his dick to behave, before rapping twice on the door jamb.

"Hi, Aiden. What's up since I saw you last?" An adorable smile hitched the corners of her mouth.

They'd driven to work together, as had become their habit, and he relished that time, using it to talk and get to know the woman she'd become. She did yoga twice a week with Amy, she still scrapbooked, though less often now, and she worked hard, often bringing paperwork home with her.

She asked him about his life abroad. He told her about the well-known places he'd visited and the countries he'd explored while at work. To his surprise, she admitted to reading some of his articles while he was gone, complimenting his skill at reporting. Her continued interest despite her anger and hurt told him she'd thought of him as often as he'd wondered about her.

He shook his head and returned to the present. "I come bearing gifts." He lifted the bag he'd held behind his back and set it on her desk. Though he'd found it just as he returned home, he'd held on to it until they'd reached a détente.

"Oh!" She smiled, her excitement obvious by how quickly she tore into the paper bag. Carefully, she pulled out the figurine and placed it in her palm. "Tinker Bell!" she all but squealed.

The small statuette sat in her hand. It was approximately five inches tall, depicting the little fairy posing with her hands on her hips, wings spread out behind her. It was cute, but that wasn't the reason he'd bought it.

Brooke stared at it for a long moment. Then, she looked up at him through her eyelashes. "You remembered," she said in a soft voice.

"As if I could forget."

"When we moved into our house, it was a couple of weeks before Halloween. You were twelve, and I was fourteen, way too old and cool to go trick-or-treating. Or so I thought."

"And I wanted to go as Tinker Bell," she mused, staring at the item in her hand.

"But you wouldn't go without Peter Pan." He vividly recalled the memory of a young Brooke, eyes filled with tears as she told her mother she couldn't be Tinker Bell without Peter Pan.

Aiden had overheard the conversation, stepping into the kitchen just as Brooke dipped her head, dejected and upset. He thought she was too old to cry over Halloween, but he'd continued to listen.

"I heard you tell your mother that your dad would have done it with you. I thought I was some tough kid, but your words broke my heart since I knew exactly how you felt."

"Because of your mom," she whispered.

He nodded, clenching his fists at his sides. Her words to her mom had hit him hard. "So I offered to step in."

Her eyes warmed at the memory. "I didn't think you'd really do it. After all, we barely knew each other, but you did. And then, you were so nice to me. Even when I tossed glitter into the air and it rained down on you, too."

"Because a fairy needed pixie dust to fly," they both said at the same time, laughing. He grinned as he slid his hands in his pockets and leaned a hip against the edge of the desk.

"I got shit for that move for weeks after. Between dressing up as a Disney character and the glitter that stuck to my hair the next day despite multiple washings, I was an easy target." He shook his head at that. "They called me fairy boy for months after that."

"Boys are so dumb. Peter Pan isn't a fairy," she said, as if that was the reason they'd made fun of him. Her lips still lifted in amusement, as she placed the figurine on her desk.

Aiden chuckled. "No regrets," he admitted. "I actually had fun that night. It was the first time you and I hung out. You were some little kid to me and I had no idea how important you'd become in my life. First as a close friend and now... much more." *So much more.*

Her eyes shifted from the figurine to him. "I had fun too. It was just the beginning of us," she mused.

He was grateful for the warmth in her eyes but more for her admission. If he'd given her the Tinker Bell figurine any earlier, she might have thrown it back in his face.

"Where did you find it?" she asked.

"I landed at JFK and was walking through the airport when I saw it in the gift shop." He'd been drawn to it like a magnet. "I was hoping every time you saw it, you'd remember that night and think of me."

Brooke swallowed hard before looking at him again, the green in her eyes appearing vibrant as they shined with emotion. "I always think of you. The memories are just a bonus, though it's taken me a long time to enjoy them instead of resenting them."

He took the hit because the change in her was so sweet. "*You* mean a lot to me, sweetheart."

She nodded. "And you to me. I'm sorry I've been so uncertain about us. I know it's time to move on from the past."

He strode around to her side of the desk and knelt beside her chair, spinning her to face him. "We said we'd date, so let's do it. Come to dinner with me tonight." They needed time alone and he just needed her.

She nodded. "Where are we going?"

"That is another surprise." He stood and pressed a kiss to her lips, savoring her taste. "Now we should get to work. I'll see you this afternoon for our meeting."

"Okay."

He walked through her office, turning as he reached her door. Brooke was staring at the figurine with soft eyes and a wistful smile.

His mood upbeat, he strode to the office he and Jared shared, noting Lara, their assistant, wasn't at her desk. And Jared was going to be late today due to an early ultrasound appointment with Charlie. Aiden walked into the empty office and sat down at his desk.

Before he could shift the mouse and awaken the desktop, he noted a simple brown envelope with his name printed on the front. It could be anything business related, but Aiden's stomach twisted as he lifted the thick manila envelope in his hand.

With trepidation, he opened it. Reaching inside, he pulled out about two dozen pictures and spread them out on his desk, taking in photos of himself in various places and poses as he went about his normal life. On the grounds at home, near the office, one even caught a stop at the grocery store for Lizzie one night this past week.

Nausea rose in his throat as he realized someone had been following him, and from the backgrounds, it looked like the person had Aiden in his sights for a while. It was creepy as hell.

As he collected the photos, he noted one had been taken in the parking lot of the strip mall. Aiden had just stepped out of the shop, a smile on his face. While he was still in a good mood about buying Brooke her chocolates, just before he was almost killed.

There was no note, no warning, threat or demand.

But spelling things out wasn't necessary. The message was clear. He was being watched, and whoever was behind the pictures wanted Aiden to know he was an easy target.

Aiden shoved them back into the envelope, opened his desk drawer, and tossed the whole package inside. Seeing those pictures reinforced the constant undercurrent of fear in his mind ever since the vehicle nearly hit him.

Anger replaced his unease. They might think he could be intimidated, but they were wrong. He had every intention of sticking to his convictions. He wouldn't back down and pull the article. They wouldn't win, no matter what they tried to do to convince him.

He considered giving the envelope to the police but knew it was a dead end. There was no way the cops would find someone stalking him in the city.

Remy would be back in less than a week and the article was due for release around the same time. Until then, he'd do his best to protect himself and those he loved. He'd keep his public outings with Brooke to a minimum and carry on as usual, while hoping for the best.

The one thing he knew he wouldn't do was expose Brooke to any danger. He'd just have to keep any public outings together to low-risk areas.

Chapter Twenty-Two

AFTER AIDEN'S VISIT to her office this morning, Brooke worried it would be difficult to focus on work during their meeting, but Aiden set a professional tone, and they were able to stay on task.

The bank that Jared wanted the company to buy wasn't large, but the potential purchase still needed to be evaluated from all angles. They spent two hours creating a one-hundred-day plan to analyze the bank's business, consult industry experts, and ultimately make an offer. The plan was just the beginning. They needed to work on assigning tasks and dates to each action item, but that could wait until tomorrow.

"That's it for today," Aiden said.

Brooke nodded. "I think we made headway."

"I agree."

She gathered her laptop and notes, and rose to her feet, but Aiden reached out and grasped her hand. His thumb pressed against the pulse point in her wrist, and she wondered if he could feel the way her heart fluttered at his touch.

"About our date. I'll pick you up at seven tonight," he said.

She wrinkled her nose in confusion. "Pick me up? We live in the same house."

He grinned. "Dress casually," he said, teasing her without explaining.

"And you still won't tell me where we're going?"

He shook his head. "Nope."

Excitement rushed through her because she loved surprises, something Aiden no doubt knew and had planned accordingly. In fact, he knew more about her than anyone. The little figurine he'd given her this morning was a reminder of both that and the good times they'd shared. Tonight, they'd share one more.

After work, she changed into jeans and a cropped top—about as casual as she could get. The evenings were balmy so she pulled her hair into a ponytail and walked downstairs. The house was empty. Her mom was out, Aiden hadn't yet come home from work, and Alex was taking a nap. Rest was the only thing the doctor ordered that he did without complaint.

The doorbell rang.

Aiden said he'd *pick her up*. At the time, she hadn't known what he meant. As she strode the rest of the way down the stairs and across the entryway, she realized he'd meant just that.

She opened the door to find Aiden standing on the front porch with a bouquet of pink peonies in his hand and a smile on his face. Despite not coming home after work, he'd changed into a pair of jeans and a soft blue T-shirt that was tight around his biceps, and the blue was a perfect contrast against his tanned skin.

He looked her over in kind, his stare going from her sneakers, up past her tight jeans, to the strip of skin between the waist and her cropped top, ending on her lightly made-up face. "You look beautiful," Aiden said, holding out the flowers. In keeping with today's theme, peonies were her favorite.

She took them and breathed in the strong, sweet scent. "Thank you. Let me put these in some water and we can leave."

Aiden followed her into the house, looking around like he'd never seen the place before. "Nice place you've got here."

Brooke chuckled, immediately realizing what his play was. He wanted to pretend they were strangers? She could do that.

"Oh, this old place? It's okay, I guess." She kept her tone flippant, even though the Sterling estate was opulent and beyond most people's means. "I just hope my luxurious way of living doesn't intimidate you. It can be a lot for a first date with someone I barely know."

Aiden grinned. "I can handle your lifestyle. I'll just try extra hard to impress you." He winked and butterflies took flight in her stomach.

After leaving the house, Aiden drove up Route 684 and pulled off an exit where she immediately saw a Ferris wheel in the background.

"We're going to a carnival?" she asked, hearing her excitement bleed through.

"What makes you think that?" he asked, laughing.

She lightly shoved his shoulder, enjoying their banter and excited about the destination. "I love that you chose this for us," she told him.

He reached over and squeezed her leg just above the knee. "Just want you to be happy," he said, and her heart swelled in her chest.

She sighed. "I am." She spoke softly but truly meant the words.

Aiden and his siblings were wealthy. They all had trust funds set up before they were born and owned shares in Sterling Investments. Aiden could afford to take a date anywhere he wanted, and he'd chosen a local carnival because it was much more her style than some expensive restaurant where she might not feel comfortable. In truth, she knew this was more his speed, too.

They parked and walked a long way to the entrance, where Aiden bought tickets for the rides and games. The place was full of people, couples, families, and friends out for a fun evening. And there were trucks selling just about every kind of fried food available, and their first stop was for footlong corn dog, which they quickly devoured.

"Oh my God," she moaned. "That was so good."

He glanced at her, eyes twinkling. "I bet you left room for fried dough and cotton candy, though."

"You know it," she said, letting out a laugh.

Aiden stopped by a tent filled with craftsmen selling art, jewelry, and hand-stitched clothing. They walked through, checking out each booth, chatting about everything and nothing. Then, they wandered over to a stage where a local rock band was performing original songs.

Brooke watched, tapping her foot to the easy beat as Aiden stepped up behind her and wrapped his arms around her waist. They stood like that for a while, listening and swaying to the music. It was easy to be with Aiden like this, to connect in a way that only old friends could. He left her for a few minutes and returned with cotton candy, just as the band took a break between sets.

While they waited, he told her some more about his travels, and it was fascinating to hear about the things he'd seen. From swimming in the Aegean to visiting monasteries in Tibet and hiking in Iceland, he'd really done it all.

"I'll admit, I'm a little jealous," she said, looking up

at him. "I haven't traveled much."

He brushed his knuckles over her cheek. "I'm not going to lie, there were times when it was amazing, but I also missed having a place to call home."

She sighed, understanding the sentiment. Brooke was a homebody and the thought of traveling such far lengths to see various sites gave her a touch of anxiety.

After they finished the cotton candy, they found an empty picnic table where they sat down so they could rest and talk more. The sun had set, and string lights hanging from the tree branches above lit the area.

"I knew journalism was your second major, but I never knew you had the desire to travel." As his close friend, she was surprised the subject had never come up.

Even if he'd made the decision to go because of misplaced guilt, there had to be a part of him drawn to that lifestyle. She'd been aware he hadn't wanted to work for the family business, and he'd spoken about the possibility of applying to magazines and newspapers in the city. If traveling was in his thoughts, why hadn't he shared that with her?

"The truth? I don't think I knew until I saw the notice for the job opening. By then, I thought it made sense to keep things to myself in case I didn't get it. Then nobody had to worry about me leaving."

"I suppose that makes sense." They were having

such a nice night, she didn't want to rehash the past.

As he spoke, he made circles on her hand with his fingers. "It wasn't a bad way to live, at least in the beginning. And I grew up a lot while I was out in the world. I learned that there are some things in life that I can't control, and that was a healthy thing for me to process and accept."

She studied his handsome profile, happy he was home now, that they were here, together. "I am glad that you found peace."

He turned her hand and clasped their palms together. "I think I found acceptance more than peace. At least when it came to my mother. As for us, that may take a little longer."

She curled her fingers around his. The walls around her heart had already begun to crumble and with each admission he made, she let him in more. "We're okay, Aiden. No more wishing for what might have been or feeling guilty. We've each accepted our part in what happened, and just maybe we weren't ready to be us back then."

His gorgeous brown eyes stared into hers. "When did you become so wise, Brooklyn Snyder?"

She laughed. "I had to grow up too. Holding on to a grudge only served to stop me from seeing the truth from all sides."

Leaning across the table, she pressed a spontaneous kiss to his lips, then lifted her head. "I think we're both wiser now." And that opened a whole host of possibilities for the future.

He slid a hand behind her neck, pulling her close. They kissed again and with each press of his lips and every electrifying stroke of his hand against her cheek, she fell for him all over again.

She just hoped he really had learned from the past and wouldn't make the same mistakes again.

Chapter Twenty-Three

By the time they left the fair, they were both exhausted. Aiden drove home, Brooke dozing in the passenger seat beside him. He'd had no hidden agenda for the night except to spend time with her and hope she had fun. He'd accomplished so much more. They'd reached a point of understanding he could only have wished for a few short weeks ago. His heart beat rapidly inside his chest at the thought of the progress they'd made together.

Brooke woke up as he pulled into the driveway, parked next to his father's car and shut off the engine.

After they exited, they walked to the back of his car and he opened the hatch to grab all her goodies in his arms. The giant stuffed bear was soft and completely impractical, but once she'd said she wanted the massive thing, he'd been determined to win the ring toss game. He'd spent more on tickets to play repeatedly than it would have cost him to buy the damn thing at a store. But when he pointed that out, she playfully accused him of trying to take the fun out of the game. Of course, she'd been right.

They walked into the house, and she locked up behind them. Aiden plopped the panda onto the living room sofa. "I think we should leave this big guy right here. Then, everyone who comes to visit will know how talented I am."

Brooke rolled her eyes. "You're such an arrogant show-off."

He flexed his biceps and grinned. "Don't act like you aren't impressed."

Her light laughter made his heart feel like it was somersaulting in his chest.

They walked upstairs, side by side. This was the part of the evening that he'd been anticipating. He knew how she felt about staying in separate rooms, but his father and Lizzie were probably sleeping, and he refused to dwell on whether they were in the same bed. Nobody would know if Brooke stayed with him and left before morning.

He paused outside their side-by-side rooms. Brooke turned to him with a shy smile on her face that made his blood run hot. She leaned against the door, and he rested one arm on the frame beside her head.

"Did you enjoy our first date?" he asked, his face close to hers.

"You know I did," she said, her words coming out on a breathless sigh. Her lips parted, and her eyes grew dark. "I had a great time."

Electricity crackled between them, his body buzzing with desire. His need had bordered on desperation before, charged by years of separation and a yearning that had seeped into his bones. What he felt now was a pulsing arousal that made him want to savor her. Every. Delectable. Inch.

"And how do you want the night to end?" he asked, all but holding his breath.

She bit down on her bottom lip, then placed her hands on his chest, running them up, over his shoulders, before hooking them around the back of his neck. "I want to end it in your bed."

She lifted onto her toes at the same time he lowered his head and their lips crashed together. He slid his tongue into her mouth, kissing her as he guided her to his room. He fumbled for the doorknob behind her until the door swung open, and they spilled into the room, breaking the kiss with laughter as they nearly fell to the floor.

They regained their footing. A soft golden light showered the room and allowed him to see everything, making him glad he'd left the lamp on his nightstand on. Brooke kicked the door shut with her foot and immediately pulled off her T-shirt and tossed it to the floor.

She wore a hot pink bra with a little bow on the front, the swells of her breasts spilling over the cups. "So fucking hot." He slid his tongue over his dry lips and as he met her gaze, her eyes glazed over with need. Without missing a beat, she shimmied out of her jeans.

The panties matched the bra, and he wondered if she'd chosen the pair with him in mind. Her dark hair was pulled back in a ponytail, and she pulled off the hair tie and brushed a hand through the locks. Her breasts swayed with the motion and all the blood in his body rushed south, his cock turning to steel.

"Are you going to just stand there watching me or strip too?" she asked.

The question kicked his mind into gear. Kicking off his shoes, he shed his clothes, leaving everything on the floor in a heap.

Her gaze on him, he grasped his erection in one hand, precum already leaking, and stroked himself while she watched. He refused to come without being inside her but holding back wasn't easy. His lazy palming of his erection had her mesmerized and he didn't want to disrupt the show.

"Take off your bra, sweetheart," he said. "I need to see all of you."

Brooke did as she was told, but she was no longer in a rush. She unhooked her bra but held it in place as the straps fell down her arms. With a playful glint in her eye, she stepped closer.

"Are you planning to be bossy all night?" she asked, looking at him like she wanted to devour him, threatening his control when he wanted this to last.

"Would you rather be in charge?" He barely recognized his own deep voice.

She smirked and gave him a small nod. "Lie down on the bed."

This wasn't what he had in mind, but he'd fucking take it. If Brooke would rather take control, he could use his mouth and hands to explore her body later.

He lay on the bed and as a reward, Brooke finally dropped the bra. She slipped out of her panties next, leaving her naked as she climbed on the bed, leaning over him. Her hair fell around her face like a curtain as she kissed his lips, then moved down his jaw. She skimmed her lips over his face, arousing him even more.

He slid his hands to her breasts, tweaking and teasing her hard, rosy nipples. He already knew she could come from this alone and doubled down on his play. But Brooke wasn't finished. She kissed her way down his chest and abs before she reached for his cock. He jerked and a sharp hiss left his lips.

But Brooke kept going. She moved down his body, kneeling between his legs. With her eyes full of promise, she held his gaze while parting her lips and dipping her head to glide her tongue around the tip. A shiver ran down his spine, his hand coming to rest in her hair.

She took him inside her mouth and all thought fled. He couldn't think and could barely breathe. Everything else became white noise. All that mattered was the raw pleasure he felt as she took him deep, the head butting up against the back of her throat.

Her hand gripped the base of his erection, and she pumped his cock, her tongue swirling around his length, as she gave him the best blow job of his life.

"Brooke." He let out a tortured sound. "I need to be inside you. Bare." He needed to feel her wet heat clasp him tight.

She released him with a wet *pop*. "I think I can manage that. I'm safe. Are you?"

He nodded and cupped her face in his hand. Eyes gleaming, she slid up his body until she straddled him, rose up on her knees, and positioned his erect cock at her entrance. She sunk down, burying his length completely.

He let out a rough groan, the feel of them truly connected one he'd never forget.

"Oh God, Aiden. You feel so good." She began to rock her hips back and forth, her breasts bouncing, her desire obviously building.

He was damn close himself. Tightening his hold on her hips, he thrust up, meeting each downward motion of her pelvis, driving him deeper.

"So fucking perfect," he muttered.

"I feel it too," she said.

As their rhythm increased, sweat slicked his skin. The sound of their bodies slapping together was erotic as hell. Aiden cupped her sensitive breasts, and she reached down, rubbing her clit, her moans coming faster.

Thank God, because he was about to explode. Pressure coiled inside him, and he grunted with each rough thrust up. "Come for me, Brooke," he commanded, taking back control. "I want to feel you pulse around my cock."

She let out a prolonged whimper. "I'm… I'm coming," she said, falling forward and catching herself with her palms on his chest. And then he felt it, the pulsing contraction of her inner walls squeezing his dick.

Her climax tipped him over the edge and with his balls drawn up tight, he came hard and long. Nothing felt as good as Brooke, him bare inside her. He never wanted it to end.

Eventually, she slid off him and lay breathing heavily on the mattress at his side. Quiet surrounded them as he caught his breath, Brooke doing the same.

Needing a connection, he reached over and grasped her hand. She intertwined their fingers, and he knew. This was it for him. No matter what happened, there was no one else. He was already aware of his feelings, but this moment cemented them in his mind.

His love for her consumed him and he almost said the words. But for her, it might be too soon. When he admitted his feelings, it had to be at a time when she would believe him. Not in the aftermath of explosive, amazing sex.

Soon, he thought. He'd tell her soon.

Chapter Twenty-Four

THE NEXT DAY at work, Aiden loaded up his briefcase with everything he would need to meet with executives at the bank they were looking to purchase.

"Are you sure you don't want me to come?" Jared asked.

"No need," Aiden assured him. "I'll have Brooke with me. Between the two of us, I'm sure we can handle it. Besides, how do you plan to go on paternity leave if you can't trust me to do the job?"

Jared held up his hands in an *I surrender* gesture. "Okay, okay. I get it. But this will be our first step into private banking, and I want it to go well."

"I understand, but you know anything unfamiliar to me Brooke can deal with. Just focus on your beautiful family. Charlie is due soon. That's what's important."

Jared grinned, some of the worry bleeding out of his features. "Yeah. She's ready for it to be done, I think. We're both eager to meet our baby girl."

Aiden put a hand on his brother's shoulder. "We all are," he said, as he closed his suitcase.

"Before you go, have you given any thought to whether you'll stay with the company after I return from leave?"

Aiden met Jared's gaze. "I'm not sure yet. You know that working here was never my dream. I appreciate that this place is a part of Dad's legacy, but I'm not sure it's the right place for me. Being behind a desk and working corporate?" He shook his head.

"I can respect that. You know I appreciate you filling in."

Aiden didn't want his brother thinking it was a burden. "I'm more than happy to help out. I'll tell you this, though. I'm not leaving home again. I'm done with that lifestyle and ready to settle down. I'm just not sure what I'll do career-wise, but travel journalism is a thing of the past."

Relief crossed Jared's features. "Good. We all missed you. Another question. Would your decision have anything to do with Brooke?"

That was something Aiden had been wanting to discuss with his sibling. He didn't want Jared finding out he and Brooke were trying to make a go of things by accident. His brother already sensed the deep history he and Brooke shared. The news shouldn't come as a surprise.

"It's as much for me as it is because of Brooke. We've been rehashing our past and trying to make things work. I have a lot to make up to her. A lot of trust to regain." And he intended to do so.

Jared grinned. "I'm happy for you both. I've always hated seeing you two so miserable around each other. You might think you've hidden things from the family, but, as I've said, we all sensed there had been something serious between you and then a big fallout. I'm just glad it's over."

"Same, big brother. Same."

Aiden left the office, meeting up with Brooke in the lobby. They took his car to the bank in Great Neck. Today was an initial meeting, a chance to introduce themselves and go over details of the bank's financial records and day-to-day operations.

Brooke was more experienced in this sort of thing, having worked closely with Jared for years, so he let her take the lead as they met with the executives. Watching her in action was illuminating. She was brilliant. She spoke with confidence and asked all the right questions. Aiden chimed in where he could, but his talents were more useful in evaluating the financial records for the bank and he had no problem acting as her second.

The meeting lasted about an hour, and when they left, they had a better insight into the bank's business.

"I think we need to go further back than two years when checking their financials," Aiden said as they walked to the car. "Just to get a better idea of how they got to this point. There's a *reason* this place is for sale, and the clearer the picture is, the better off we'll be. I'd rather cover our asses now than play catch-up later."

"I agree," Brooke said.

He glanced at his watch, noting it was almost noon. "Do you want to grab lunch before we head back to work?"

"Sure. On our drive here, I saw a diner about a mile away," Brooke said.

Aiden nodded. "Sounds good."

The diner was easy to spot, and he pulled into the lot and parked. Once inside, the restaurant was just like any other roadside diner, from the black-and-white checkered tiles to the red vinyl booths and chrome-lined counter.

The lunchtime rush was in full force, but they managed to snag a table not far from the entrance. Brooke took the wall seat and they each placed their briefcases on the extra chairs. They'd decided to bring their work into the restaurant should they needed to refer to a document when discussing today's meeting.

A waitress arrived immediately. "Can I get you two something to drink?" she asked.

"I think we're ready to order. Aiden?" Brooke asked.

He nodded but waited for her to go first.

Brooke grinned as she ordered. "I'll have the burger deluxe and a chocolate milkshake."

He laughed because she did love her chocolate. "I'll take the same burger deluxe and a Coke."

"Got it," the middle-aged woman said. "I'll be back with your drinks first." She strode away, leaving them alone.

Brooke leaned back in her seat. "Between the fair and today's meal, I'm going to have to go to hot yoga to work off these calories."

"I guess I'm a bad influence but from where I'm sitting, you're perfect."

Heat flared in her eyes. "Thank you, you charmer, you."

He was grateful for her new, easy demeanor and how well things seemed to be going between them. They talked about the meeting and their next steps until the waitress returned with their drinks.

Brooke placed a straw in her tall glass and began to suck down her shake.

Their meals came next, and they finished their burgers quickly. Brooke patted her mouth with her napkin. "Excuse me. I'll be right back." She slid from the booth and walked to the back of the diner where the restrooms were located.

Aiden paid the bill at the table, then glanced at his

phone, checking his mail while waiting for Brooke to return. A man approached, catching Aiden's attention, but he ignored him, focusing instead on returning an important email from one of the bank execs he'd just met.

A hand reached out and grabbed his briefcase. Aiden glanced up as the man ran for the nearby front door.

"Hey!" he shouted, drawing attention from everyone seated nearby, as he jumped up from his seat and followed the man.

A waitress crossed in front of him with a large tray in her hands and before he could catch up with the thief, the man had disappeared out the front door. Aiden stumbled around the woman without bumping into her and by the time he rushed out of the exit, all he saw was a black SUV peeling out of the parking lot.

"Shit!" he shouted.

"Aiden? What's wrong?" Brooke asked, rushing out the front of the diner as she asked.

He hadn't gotten a good look at the man, and the license plate on the SUV had been covered. Once again, no proof. No evidence. Despite it all, he couldn't let this go.

He glanced at Brooke. "We need to call the police. Someone stole my briefcase."

Her eyes opened wide. "What?"

He nodded.

She slipped her hand into his and waited as he made the call.

Twenty minutes later, he and Brooke were crammed into the small space of the manager's office, a police officer holding up a far wall. The diner manager had pulled the security footage and they watched it on the computer. The camera didn't show Aiden's table but it had picked up a man in a black shirt, hat pulled down low on his forehead, walking in that direction just before Aiden's briefcase, with his laptop inside, was taken.

"He has to be the one who stole it," Aiden muttered.

"Any outside cameras?" the police officer asked.

The manager shook his head. "No, sorry." He shoved his hands into his pockets. "Can I get back out there? We have a big lunch crowd."

The officer nodded and the man left, leaving the three of them alone in the office.

"Mr. Sterling, I'm afraid we're not going to get much information from this." He shut the computer. "If you want to come down to the station, we can fill out a report, but I'm not hopeful anything will come of it."

Despite his anger and frustration, Aiden agreed. "Never mind. Thanks for coming."

The man inclined his head. "Part of the job. I'm just sorry I couldn't help."

Beside him, Brooke sighed. "So frustrating!"

He squeezed her hand in silent appreciation.

Aiden might not know much, but he was sure this was tied to the article. No doubt he was being followed, and the black SUV had to be the one that almost ran him down in the parking lot. They were looking for the article. But what the people behind this didn't know was that his work laptop, which was in the stolen briefcase, wasn't the same as his personal one. That was locked in his father's safe in the house. The only other copy of the article was with John and the paper. He was too paranoid to back it up on the cloud.

Still, this move felt desperate, and that worried him. Desperation could lead people to do dangerous things.

Aiden put an arm around Brooke, holding her close, and reminded himself it wasn't much longer. The article would be published in a few days. The optimist in him hoped all of this would be over but he was aware of the potential for revenge. At some point, he might need an alternative plan.

Chapter Twenty-Five

A FEW DAYS after the incident at the diner, Brooke, Aiden, Alex, and her mom were sitting at the dining room table at Aiden's father's house. Alex sat at the head with Brooke's mom to his right. Aiden and Brooke were across from her.

"I've got to tell you, Lizzie," Aiden said, spearing a piece of asparagus on his fork, "I missed your cooking while I was gone."

Brooke's mom laughed. "You always were a charmer, Aiden Sterling."

Aiden's eyes flickered over to Brooke, and he smirked, probably because she'd called him the same thing the other day. She rolled her eyes but couldn't fight off her own smile.

"What do you think of the food, Dad?" Aiden asked with the slightest hint of teasing in his voice.

Alex picked at his meal, his brow furrowed as he stared down at his plate, as if the lean chicken and grilled vegetables had personally offended him.

At Aiden's question, he looked up and gave Lizzie an obviously fake smile. "It's great, Lizzie, as always."

Brooke stuffed a bite of skinless chicken breast

into her mouth and stifled the urge to giggle. Her mom really was a great cook, but before his second heart attack and dietary restrictions, he loved unhealthy food. His favorite food was bacon, which probably had a lot to do with his clogged arteries.

But it was sweet of him to act like he enjoyed the healthier meal her mother worked hard to prepare. Brooke saw her mom reach out to squeeze his hand, and he sent her a look full of warmth and affection.

Happiness filled her. When her dad died years ago, they'd both been devastated. She thought her mom might never move on, but slowly, over time, feelings started to develop between Lizzie and Alex.

Despite her mother's attempt to hide the beginning of their relationship, it was impossible for Brooke to miss the lingering looks and casual touches they shared. Two years ago, they revealed the truth. Brooke hadn't been surprised. Some of the Sterling kids were but everyone cared about her mother and were pleased they'd both found happiness together.

"So, the plumber will start excavating the day after tomorrow?" Alex asked, as he reluctantly scooped some brown rice onto his fork.

The plumber had been delayed on another ongoing job and Aiden hadn't been eager to rush him, either. "Yes. It'll take a couple of days, but he stopped by and used a sewer scope to locate the problem, so the damage to the yard should be minimal."

"That's good to hear," Alex said.

Brooke's mom cleared her throat, and all eyes turned her way. "I need to tell you all something." She placed her napkin on the table and folded her hands together, no smile on her face.

"Mom, what's wrong?" Brooke asked, her mother's serious expression worrying her.

"Nothing!" Lizzie rushed to say. "It's just that when the work on the gatehouse is complete, I won't be moving back in there." Her apologetic gaze slid to Brooke.

"You're moving in here?" Aiden asked, while Brooke tried to process the implications.

"Yes, she is," Alex said.

"Only if you're both okay with it." Her mother said in a no-nonsense voice.

How *did* Brooke feel about her mom taking such a big step? Not that it mattered. Lizzie was entitled to live where and how she wanted.

And when she let the news settle? "I'm thrilled for you both," Brooke said, aware her voice held all the warmth she felt for them.

Her mom smiled, then turned her gaze to Aiden. "And you?" she asked.

He reached for her mother's hand. "You don't need my permission to move in here," he said. "This is my dad's house and his life. I want you both to be happy." He smiled at her before releasing his grip. "Besides, I'm only living here temporarily."

Brooke glanced at him, her stomach suddenly in knots. Was he leaving again when Jared returned to work?

"What is your plan, son?" Alex asked.

"When I first came home, I wasn't sure what my future plans were and I wanted to spend time with you." He turned his gaze to Brooke. "Now that I've decided I plan to stay home for good, I'll start looking for my own place."

She exhaled a long, relieved breath. Though he'd once again announced something huge in front of the family without telling her privately, this was very good news. News she'd have to trust in. A lot of changes had been revealed in one short family meal.

The mood was light and happy as they finished dinner. When the meal wrapped up, Lizzie recruited Alex for clean up, and sent Brooke and Aiden into the living room to relax. Or so she said. Brooke had a feeling her mother was giving them time alone. Though Brooke hadn't had a private moment to tell her mother she and Aiden were dating, as she'd already learned, a mother sensed some things.

She followed Aiden into the living room, taking a seat on the couch. He settled in beside her, ignoring the space on the other side.

He slid an arm over the back cushion, behind her head, and turned to face her. "Now that your mom isn't moving back into the gatehouse, are you going to stay?" he asked.

She shook her head. "I've been thinking it was time to move into my own place anyway. I have the money saved and I only stayed as long as I did so Mom wasn't alone. She clearly doesn't need my company anymore," she said with a wry grin.

"So I guess we're both looking for a new place to live."

Her breath hitched at his words. Could he be hinting at them moving in together?

Before he could continue, his cell rang. He groaned, pulled the phone from his back pocket, and slid his finger across the screen to answer the call. "Jared? Everything okay?"

Brooke couldn't hear his reply but Aiden's sexy lips turned upward in a huge grin. "Okay, great. Brooke and I will be there right away." He tapped the off button and met her gaze.

"Charlie's in labor?" she asked, feeling the excitement as she spoke.

"She sure is. I need to tell Dad."

They rose to their feet at the same time Alex walked out of the kitchen, her mother alongside him.

"Jared called."

"I just heard," Aiden said. "Two cars or one?" he asked his father.

"Let's take two in case anyone wants to leave early," Lizzie suggested.

Aware her mother would be the one dragging Alex out if the night went on too long and he got too tired, she stifled a laugh and nodded.

"Sounds good," Aiden said.

When they arrived at the hospital and made their way to the waiting room, the rest of the Sterling siblings had already arrived. Even Remy and Raven, who had just returned from vacation were there.

"Where's Dad?" Dex asked as they joined the crowd.

"Dad and Lizzie are on their way," Aiden said.

"Is there any news?" Brooke asked, turning to Fallon and Noah.

She shrugged. "I don't know. We just got here, too. I had to get Aunt Clara to stay with Gabbi," she said of her former boss, now partner at the gallery they co-owned. The twins were huddled together in the corner, bouncing with excitement.

"Not yet," Remy said, joining them. "We were with them when her water broke and drove them to the hospital. Jared said Charlie's contractions were only five minutes apart by the time we arrived."

The next hour consisted of everyone hanging out in the waiting room, eager for the arrival of the newest member of their family. Remy left to meet Alex and Lizzie at the entrance of the hospital and bring them to join the family. Aiden kept the twins entertained with wild stories of his worldly adventures. Though Brooke was sure he exaggerated most of them, the girls were fascinated. Noah was busy on his phone, and Dex was in a corner with Samantha, their heads together as they talked in low voices. And Brooke listened to Fallon and Raven chat while taking in the warmth of the scene around her, grateful to be part of it.

The automatic doors leading to the delivery rooms opened and Jared stepped into the room, a dazed look in his eyes. "Kylie Gigi Sterling has arrived! We named her after both our moms."

Brooke glanced at Alex, who had tears in his eyes. "That's wonderful news." She turned to Aiden who'd stepped up beside her and pulled her into a hug.

Jared's happiness spread through the waiting room, and everyone rushed forward to congratulate him, making it quick because he was eager to get back to Charlie and the new baby.

They waited for a chance to see the new family and finally, Jared reappeared, ushering them in a few at a time, starting with the twins. He wrapped an arm around each girl and led them out the door and toward their mom and new sister.

Seeing the tender happiness that they shared made Brooke think about her own future. She wanted this one day; the love, the babies, and a husband who looked at her like she hung the moon.

Before she could think on that further, it was their time to go in to see the family. Charlie was exhausted but glowing. Jared hovered like a new dad.

And Aiden sat in the visitor's chair, cradling his niece in his arms. He looked up at her, warmth and other emotions in his eyes, and she knew. He was the only person she wanted this kind of future with.

The longing she felt in that moment was so overwhelming she teared up, accepting the inevitable. No one made her as happy as Aiden Sterling. No one had ever made her as miserable, either. But love took work. Both parties had to try their best. Though Aiden had shattered her years ago, he was still the only person who could make her feel whole. Which meant she had put the past behind her. She believed that Aiden wouldn't hurt her again.

And that set her free.

Chapter Twenty-Six

THE FAMILY STAYED at the hospital until visiting hours ended. The nursing staff all but had to kick them out. Everyone was so thrilled about the new baby and Aiden was right there with them.

But it wasn't just the new addition to the family that put him in a good mood. As they walked across the hospital lobby, Brooke at his side, she intertwined her fingers with his. They were together. Though they still needed to talk about their relationship and what it would look like, to him, that was just a technicality. He wasn't going anywhere, ever again.

As they stepped out of the hospital and into the night, Aiden paused. The asphalt was wet from rain, which obviously started sometime while they'd been inside.

Beside him, Brooke stilled and stared out at the dark night. "I hate heavy rain," she said.

"I know, sweetheart. But it's not icy and I can handle the short drive home."

Ever since her father died on icy roads at night, driving in bad weather made her nervous. Even rain.

"I'll drive slow. I promise." He glanced at her.

"Ready?"

She nodded and as he walked forward, she fell into step alongside him.

He drove home with more caution than ever. Her tension got to him and he didn't want her any more upset than she already was. He hated to think of her handling these drives alone all these years, but it did no good for him to look back now.

Glancing from the corner of his eye he saw her hands gripping her seat belt tightly, her leg bouncing up and down with nervous energy. "We'll be home soon," he promised. And to distract her, he said, "I hope you weren't planning to sleep in your own bed tonight, because I want you with me."

She let out a huff of unexpected laughter. "Really? You're trying to make me focus on something else by talking about sex?"

"No." He pulled up to a red light and glanced at her with a smile. "I'm saying that I want you in my arms tonight. I don't like seeing you so scared, and it's driving me crazy."

"Well, we're just a couple blocks from home."

He took her hand and pressed a kiss to the back, just as the light changed. The green arrow appeared and he began his left turn, moving slowly as there was no one behind him, and he knew this light gave him plenty of time.

Out of nowhere, a dark vehicle darted out from the parking lot across the street, screeching into the road and gunning it toward them. The SUV came closer and it resembled the vehicle that nearly ran him over and fled from the diner.

"Shit!" he shouted, and shot his arm out to brace Brooke even as he slammed his foot down on the brakes. Their car shot forward, hitting a puddle and hydroplaning out of control.

Brooke screamed, the shrill sound ringing in his ears as everything blurred around him. Every muscle in his body seized tight and he attempted to maneuver the vehicle out of the spin and bring the car to a stop.

He whipped his neck to the side in time to see the SUV speed off. As for them, the car had spun a few times and come to a stop, one tire over the sidewalk.

"Brooke?" He looked at her terror-filled face, eyes wide, skin pale, and her body trembling.

Tears swam in her eyes, but she didn't answer him. He unbuckled himself first, then reached over and did the same for her, pulling her into his arms as best he could in the front seat. She sniffed into his shirt, and he whispered soothing words in her ear, all the while running a hand up and down her back, comforting her as much as possible.

But inside, he was *furious.*

Chapter Twenty-Seven

THE NEXT MORNING, Brooke sat in the kitchen with her mom, a cup of coffee in hand. She hadn't slept well last night, the near accident leaving her too rattled to get any rest. By the time the police came and took their statements, it was late. Once home, she'd let her mother make her a cup of tea to help her relax.

But when she lay down, even wrapped in Aiden's protective arms, sleep eluded her. And when she managed to finally fall asleep, a nightmare about the incident startled her awake. The pattern repeated itself until the morning sun came in through the windows.

A glance at the clock on the microwave told her it was just after ten a.m. She was tired and anxious, her stomach still rolling too much for her to eat or hold food down.

She'd known since the night she'd seen his hands wrapped in bandages that something was going on with Aiden, and she had no doubt last night was related, as well. Because that SUV had been *trying* to hit them. She was sure the briefcase theft was another thing she could chalk up to whatever was going on with him.

"You look like you need this," Brooke's mom said, placing a fresh, hot cup of coffee on the kitchen island in front of her.

"Thanks, Mom." She pushed aside the cold cup and added both milk and sugar to the new one. Taking a long sip, then another, the warmth helped and she hoped the jolt of caffeine would kick in soon.

Aiden was in the living room with his father, waiting for the rest of the siblings to come to the house. Aiden had something to share with everyone. And though he'd offered to tell her prior, she had chosen to take the time to pull herself together and hear it along with everyone else. She did appreciate him giving her the choice this time, before he made another family announcement.

Jared was the only sibling not coming today. Charlie was still in the hospital with the baby, and though they'd discharge her later today, he didn't want to leave her side.

"How's your chest feel?" her mom asked as Brooke drank her coffee.

"It's sore," Brooke said, wincing. Bruises had settled across her chest from the seat belt tightening as the car had spun out of control. "I'm still in shock."

Her mom nodded. "I'm curious to hear what Aiden has to say. He didn't tell you what's going on?"

She shook her head. "I opted to wait for the rest of the family."

The last time he'd made an announcement to the group, he'd broken her heart, but they'd reached the point where she could give him the benefit of the doubt.

"Let's go see who's here," Brooke said. Taking her coffee, she and her mom walked into the crowded living room.

The vibe was completely different from last night at the hospital. By now, they all knew about the accident and knew it was the catalyst for this meeting. Still, the murmurs and question why reverberated around her.

The living room was large enough to seat everyone, but Brooke hesitated. Aiden was standing in front of his family, his obvious nerves causing his hands to jangle in front of him.

She met his gaze, and he extended an arm, encouraging her to join him. Something loosened in her chest as she strode toward him, the lingering fear of what came next no longer so strong.

He wrapped his arm around her waist in front of his family. Most of the Sterlings seemed unfazed. Brooke might have laughed about the way they already knew there was something going on between her and Aiden, but the seriousness of this situation kept her somber.

Aiden drew a deep breath and squeezed her close. "I have something I need to explain, and I know it's going to be upsetting. I just ask that you wait until you know everything before we discuss it."

A few of his siblings nodded, but no one said a word.

Aiden spoke for the next twenty minutes, revealing a story that began while he'd been abroad. The piece he'd been investigating. The death of his informant, leading to the desire to give up the job he once loved. How Jared needing him at Sterling Investments came at the right time. And the fact that he'd hoped returning to the States would end the harassment from abroad.

It hadn't. And then everything she'd wondered about became clear. All three incidents were tied to the threats he'd received. Threats he told none of them about. Oh, he'd mentioned a dangerous story to her. And she'd been foolish enough not to push for more information.

Anger lanced through her. He'd opted to go through these traumatizing events alone. They'd had so many deep conversations as they reconnected, talking about trust, and he hadn't said a word. A glance around the room told her his siblings were just as furious.

"What the hell, Aiden?" Fallon snapped, and Noah

put a comforting arm around her. Or maybe he was trying to keep her on the couch because she looked like she was about to jump to her feet.

But Raven, Remy's wife, couldn't keep her husband seated, and he faced Aiden with a narrowed gaze. "Why the hell didn't you tell me? You know damn well I have connections in the police department, and I could have had a protective detail put on you."

Aiden released his hold on Brooke, and she stepped away, not wanting to make this about her. Obviously, Aiden was dealing with a lot, and now he had his upset family to calm down.

"I should have told you sooner," Aiden said, his eyes meeting Brooke's before taking in the rest of his family. "At first, I wasn't sure if it was a serious threat. Or maybe I didn't want to believe it had followed me back here."

"Someone tried to run you over in a parking lot!" Dex shouted, and Fallon nodded her head hard.

"Because they want to stop the article from going to print. It's being released tomorrow, and I had hoped the threat would disappear afterward. They'll be too busy doing cleanup to worry about me." He repeated his editor's words, now wondering if that had been naïve.

Remy glared at Aiden, a combination of anger and fear in his eyes. He'd always been protective and realizing that Aiden had been in danger for weeks would no doubt tear him up. Especially because he'd been kept in the dark.

Brooke understood the feeling.

"Haven't you ever heard of *retribution*?" Dex asked through clenched teeth. "These people might be pissed off enough to try to kill you whether the article is out there or not."

"Dex has a point, son," Alex said, his skin pale and the deep lines of his face more prominent than usual.

"I thought about it, I just hoped things would end with publication," Aiden said. He glanced at his father and his shoulders sagged, no doubt because he realized the stress this was putting on Alex.

"I guess I wanted to believe I'd be home free afterward and that's why I kept quiet. But once Brooke was in the car with me, it became clear no one around me was safe."

Everyone began talking at once.

Aiden tried to explain himself, while Remy asked for more details, and Fallon began to cry. Dex and Samantha were talking to each other, and it seemed like she was trying to calm him down. There was so much noise, and the emotions running wild were suffocating.

Brooke needed space so she slipped out of the room. Walking through the kitchen, she opened the sliding glass door and stepped out onto the patio in the backyard. She couldn't stop the truth from running in her head on a constant loop. He'd been trying to win her back for weeks, all the while being threatened by some unknown enemy.

Taking a deep breath, she closed her eyes and tried to think clearly. Him keeping this huge secret was a tough pill to swallow but she couldn't help but think he'd avoided telling her about it for a reason. Because he didn't think she was strong enough to handle it? Because he was worried she'd back away if she knew? Either way, he hadn't given her enough credit, and they'd be having words later. This seemed like another example of him taking a choice away from her and making decisions on his own.

In the past, she'd have let the hurt consume her and push him away, but she'd learned her lesson. Running didn't bring her peace or happiness. Being with Aiden did. And now she felt a little better after her few minutes of introspection.

She was just about to head back inside when the door opened, and her mom stepped out.

She gave Brooke a small smile, placing a hand on her shoulder. "Are you okay?"

Brooke chuckled but there was no humor in it. "Not really."

"Of course you aren't. It was a silly question. You

just found out your boyfriend's life is being threatened."

"Exactly."

Her mom tucked a strand of hair behind Brooke's ear. "We haven't really had much of a chance to talk lately, but I had a feeling something was going on between you two again."

"You've always been clever." Brooke gripped her mom's arm and gave it a squeeze. "I'm sorry I didn't tell you before now. It's just been... complicated."

"I understand that. My journey with Alex wasn't exactly straightforward, either. But I've known about your feelings for Aiden for years now. You can't hide that kind of thing from your mom."

Brooke pulled her mother into a hug. She'd held back her feelings for Aiden for so long, it felt good to talk about this with her. "I never wanted anyone to have to pick sides," she admitted.

"Well, I'm not just anyone, but I know you. And I was there for you, supporting you, whether you told me or not."

"I love you, Mom."

"Me too, baby girl." She kissed the top of Brooke's head. "Ready to go inside?"

Brooke nodded. Rising, they walked back into the house. There were no longer voices shouting over each other, and Brooke let out a relieved breath.

Maybe they could figure out a plan together.

She stepped into the living room to see only Aiden and Remy were still in the room, their backs facing her.

"You're right. I don't know if the threat will go away once the article comes out," Aiden said, unaware she was in the room. "I only have one choice. I have to leave New York."

Chapter Twenty-Eight

AIDEN RAN A frustrated hand through his hair, angry with himself and the situation he found himself in. He'd wanted to come home and move on, so despite the threats and warnings, it had been too hard to accept the fact that he was truly unsafe.

He could see now, he'd performed some damned good mental gymnastics to convince himself he'd be okay if he could just hold on until the article was published. He'd been in complete denial about the danger.

Until Brooke was in the car with him when the SUV tried to hit them. Her scream still echoed in his ears and brought reality home to him. She could have been killed, and it would have been his fault. He hadn't been worried enough about himself, but he loved Brooke too much to risk her life ever again.

He'd held her all night, not catching any sleep because he knew what he had to do when morning came. Starting with telling his family and Brooke about his reality and the risk he posed to them all.

After everyone finished yelling, his father had ushered them all out, insisting Aiden and Remy come up with a reasonable plan. After listening to his oldest brother tear him a new one for not reaching out to him, *to hell with his vacation*, he realized he'd been living in a fantasy world.

Dex had been right, too. *"Haven't you ever heard of retribution?"*

Aiden had no idea what would or wouldn't motivate someone to come for him, be it to stop him from publishing the article or for payback because he hadn't. Would they come for him? His family? Brooke?

He had to leave so the people he loved didn't have targets on their backs.

Turning to Remy, who had suggested he leave town, he said, "You're right. I don't know if the threat will go away once the article comes out. I only have one choice. I have to leave New York."

A gasp sounded behind him and he spun around to see Brooke staring at him in wide-eyed disbelief. "What did you just say?"

Shit, shit, and double shit. "Brooke, listen." He intended to explain everything in detail so she understood he had no alternative.

"No, I will not listen. You are not leaving when you just decided to stay." She set her hands on her hips and glared at him.

God, she was beautiful in her fury. His girl had

found her voice. Unlike five years ago when he'd dictated how things would be, today, she stood up to him and he admired the hell out of her for doing so.

"Brooke…" He reached for her, but she took a step back.

"Do not try and placate me," she warned him.

"I have to leave so everyone, including you, will be safe. But it's temporary and I'll come back when the threat is gone. I swear." His heart hammered hard in his chest, but she needed to let him do what was right. He'd put everyone at risk for too long.

She narrowed her gaze, her suspicion clear. "And when will that be?" she asked.

Remy cleared his throat and met her gaze. "Based on what we know about the corruption that Aiden will expose in the article, I think he's right about the country involved launching an investigation. But the idea that the people behind all this will disappear because the article ran is flawed."

Brooke bit down on her lower lip.

Aiden used her silence to speak. "It'll take time for the people responsible for both the corruption and Ingrid's death to be held accountable. Until then, everyone will be safer away from me. I can lay low somewhere they can't find me." He hated the idea of being alone somewhere, hiding out away from his family and away from Brooke. "Think of it like witness protection."

Brooke glared at him.

"That means no contact, doesn't it?" Lizzie asked.

Aiden hadn't realized her mother had walked into the room, his father's arm around her shoulders.

"Yes," Aiden said. There was no use lying or hedging the question. "But Remy promised to move heaven and earth to get this situation resolved quickly."

She turned to the oldest Sterling sibling. "How long will that take?" Her words sounded more like a demand.

Remy rubbed his hand over his stubbled jaw. "It's hard to say. I think it's clear that these are some powerful people we're dealing with. Taking them down could take weeks… months…"

"Years?" she asked in a hollow voice.

"Maybe," Remy admitted.

"No. Absolutely not," Brooke said.

If he hadn't convinced her by now, he never would. "I have to do this, so there's no point in further discussion."

Shooting an apologetic glance at everyone, he walked out of the room, leaving his heart behind him. It killed him to think about leaving them, especially Brooke, but keeping them safe was his priority.

He stormed up the stairs to his bedroom and started to pack.

Chapter Twenty-Nine

BROOKE PACED THE living room in an attempt to calm down. Again. She'd convinced her mother and Alex to give her space to think, and Remy went to find Raven, who had gone to the den to wait.

Alone, she understood Aiden needed to protect the people he loved, but he was forgetting one very important thing, and she had every intention of sharing it with him.

Brooke stormed to his bedroom, a woman on a mission. She was so done with Aiden's lone wolf crap and she wouldn't let him have his way again.

Fueled by her anger, she shoved his door open and didn't care when it banged into the wall.

Aiden spun around from where he stood by the bed, folding clothes into a large suitcase. "Brooke?"

She slammed the door shut behind her and leaned against the white wood. "Let me make something clear to you, Aiden. You took charge of my life once and I am not letting you do it again."

His jaw clenched before he let himself speak. "I've made up my mind."

"Oh, I'm aware. So you're packing already?" she asked.

"Yes. I'm leaving in the morning." He picked up another shirt and folded it, placing the garment in the suitcase.

"I see."

He faced her, narrowing his gaze, his wrinkled brow showing his confusion. She knew he expected a shouting match, but that wasn't what she planned to give him.

Strolling over to where he stood, she folded her arms across her chest and tilted her head to the side. "Okay, where are we going?"

He was in the process of tucking a pair of well-worn jeans into the suitcase when her question obviously registered. Pausing with the jeans in his hands, he looked at her with his eyebrows drawn together, creating a crease in his forehead.

He was clearly still a confused man. "Did you just say *we*?" he asked.

Brooke treated him to a patronizing smile. "I certainly did."

Aiden groaned, running his hand through his hair. "Brooke, I can't take you with me."

She realized he looked bone-deep tired. Not just sleep-deprived like her, but emotionally depleted, and she understood the feeling.

But she wasn't backing down. They were in this together. "Why not?"

"For one thing, I don't know how long I'll be gone, and like I said, I'll need to cut contact. With everyone. I won't rip you away from your life just because my actions have put me in danger."

And here it was. The old Aiden coming out to play. Instead of allowing her anger to overwhelm her, she faced him, stepping into his personal space. "Aiden Sterling, are you trying to make decisions for me again?" she asked, her voice harsher than she'd intended.

He jerked his head back and she saw him as he put the pieces together in his mind.

But she had no patience for him to figure it out. "I refuse to let you decide what is best for me again. And before you try it, you're not going to push me away, either. I'm not that insecure girl you left behind once before. I love you too much to let you go without a fight. And this time, I know you love me, too." Shocked by her own declaration, she clamped her mouth shut.

But she shouldn't be so surprised. Aiden was the one person who could make her forget herself. And now that she'd said the words? She wouldn't take them back.

She stood firm, holding her breath, waiting for his reaction. Expecting the argument that he couldn't drag her with him away from her home, family, and job.

Instead, he closed the distance between them, wrapped his arms around her, and kissed her long, hard, and deep. His tongue tangled with hers, giving her the answer he hadn't yet said.

His hands traveled down, cupping her ass and lifting her so she could wrap her arms around his neck and her legs around his waist.

Once he had her in place, he tilted his head back long enough to say the words. "You're right, sweetheart. I love you, too."

After that, she fell sideways on the bed with Aiden beside her, still kissing and pulling at each other's clothes. He shoved the suitcase onto the floor and kissed her again, her body clamoring for his touch.

Rolling her onto her back, he settled his hips between her parted thighs. Somehow, she'd managed to strip down to her panties. Aiden's shirt was gone, leaving him in his jeans. The rough fabric abraded against her sex as the hard ridge of his erection rubbed her in just the right spot.

She jerked at the arousing feeling, needing more. He broke their kiss, and Aiden licked his way down her chest, flicking his tongue over one taut nipple, his hand squeezing the other breast. The sensations were delicious and completely overwhelming.

She grabbed his belt buckle, unbuttoning his pants and reaching inside to grasp his cock in her palm.

Aiden let out a low groan and took her mouth in another kiss, this one a sloppy, frenzied connection of lips, teeth, and tongue. She'd never felt anything like the wildness between them.

She stroked his hard length, giving the head a squeeze that made him shudder. Without warning, he yanked her panties to the side and slipped two fingers inside of her.

He groaned, burying his face in her neck. His warm breath added another layer of sensation, and she admitted to herself, the man was addictive. "You're so wet and ready for me, aren't you?" he asked, flicking his tongue over her nipple.

"Oh, yes." She undulated her hips around his fingers, her inner walls squeezing him tight.

With a sexy grin on his handsome face, he pulled his fingers out and brought them to his mouth, holding her gaze as he sucked them clean.

Damn, this man was hot. "Get your jeans off," she insisted, pushing at the waistband.

He rolled to the side and maneuvered out of them along with his boxer briefs. Once he was naked, she hooked one leg around his hips, pulling him closer. Her hands explored every inch of his hard body while he positioned himself at her entrance and pushed deep inside.

He filled her, the incredible feeling overwhelming

her. She let out a loud moan and he covered her mouth with his hand. "Shh. The parents," he reminded her.

Alex's room was on the other side of the house, and she didn't want to think of her mother's love life any more than her mother would want to consider Brooke's. But on the off chance they were still downstairs, she needed to remain silent.

She licked his palm and laughed, and he released his hand. "Behave," he said, pressing a kiss to first one side of her mouth, then the other.

"Are you going to move anytime soon?" She arched her lower back, feeling like she sucked him in deeper.

In response, Aiden pulled out, then drove into her hard and fast. He pumped his hips, slamming inside her over and over, the movements bringing her higher and closer to a climax. She raked her nails down his back.

Her voice grew hoarse as she urged him on. "Faster, harder," she groaned, unable to stifle her moans and desperate cries. The bed creaked and sweat made their bodies slick. Pleasure coiled inside her, her legs shook, and she was so close.

Then Aiden was gone, leaving her clenching around nothing. In shock, she opened her eyes to find him looming over her. He grasped her hips and flipped her over. In desperation, she climbed to her hands and knees just as he entered her once more.

Gripping her hips tight, he pounded into her from behind, reaching places inside her she'd never been touched before. Everything in her coiled tight, her body on the precipice, ready to fly.

"Aiden, I'm so close." He thrust harder again and again. "Oh God, I'm almost there."

He leaned forward, his sweat-slickened chest pressed against her back, his hips thrusting in and out. He brought his hand around her waist and slid his finger over her swollen clit, rubbing with firm pressure.

She let go then, bright lights flashing behind her eyes as her entire being imploded. She came hard, Aiden's name on her lips.

He followed close behind, the band of his arm tightening around her waist, his climax overtaking him. They lay together until he finally pulled out, and she collapsed on the bed, his big frame falling onto the mattress beside her. His heavy breath sounded in her ear while she gasped to catch her own. Never in her life had she ever been so satisfied.

Aiden clasped her hand in his and brought it to his lips, pressing a kiss to the pulse point in her wrist. "You win," he said in a rough voice. "We'll leave together in the morning."

Smiling, she cuddled into his side. She might not know what the future held, but at least they would experience it together.

Chapter Thirty

AIDEN WOKE UP slowly, a shrill sound pulling him out of a deep sleep, with the woman he loved snuggled in his arms. Brooke stirred, and he looked around for his damned phone.

He grabbed it from the nightstand. His editor's name flashed on the screen. He picked up the phone, causing Brooke to groan and roll over.

"John?" Aiden asked, his voice rough from sleep.

"Aiden, sorry to bother you. I just wanted to let you know that the FBI reached out to me."

Aiden glanced at his phone screen, noting they'd slept in. It was nearly ten in the morning. "The article went out this morning?"

At the mention of his piece, Brooke pushed herself to a sitting position, her eyes wide as she listened to his side of the conversation. He braced a hand on her thigh as he and John spoke.

"As planned," John said. "In both the online publication of the magazine and on grocery store shelves and newsstands. Subscribers should have gotten them in their inboxes first thing this morning."

"And the FBI?" Aiden asked. "Are they asking

about the content?" Aiden sat upright in bed.

"I assume so, but I don't know yet," John said. "The agent I spoke with wants to talk to us both. Can you come to the magazine's office for a meeting?"

"Sure thing. I'll see you soon." He glanced at Brooke.

"You need to go meet with John?" she asked.

"Actually, John and the FBI."

Her eyes opened wide. "The FBI? Why?"

Sensing her anxiety, he grasped her hand. "That's what I need to find out. Wait here and I'll come back. By then, Remy will have us set up with somewhere to lay low for a while."

Swallowing hard, she nodded. "Okay. That's fine."

Aware the brave attitude was a façade, he leaned in and pressed a kiss to her lips. "Everything will be okay. While I'm gone, go ahead and pack your things."

She treated him to a forced smile. "I can do that."

He showered, then dressed and headed to the magazine's office, checking for a tail along the way. Since his work was mostly on the road, Aiden hadn't been here often over the years, but he knew where he was going. He parked in the garage and met up with John in the lobby, breathing a sigh of relief that his trip had ended without incident.

He shook his mentor's hand.

"They're waiting in the conference room," John

said, leading him to an elevator and once inside, he pressed the button for the eleventh floor.

They walked to the conference room where a man in a black suit was waiting, a serious expression on his face.

"Mr. Sterling, thank you for joining us," he said, rising and holding out his hand. "I'm Agent Jessop."

Aiden shook his hand, then he and John took a seat across the table. Clasping his hands, Aiden waited for the man to speak.

"I think you both know why we're here," Agent Jessop said. "We need to discuss the article you released this morning."

Aiden wasn't surprised but he would let his boss take the lead.

"Does the FBI usually respond this swiftly to accusations of corruption in a foreign country?" John asked. "The article has only been out for a few hours."

The agent shook his head. "No. You're right in assuming the wheels of government move slowly. But in this case, you've stumbled upon information that is relevant to an already ongoing investigation."

Aiden leaned forward, his interest piqued. "What investigation would that be?"

Agent Jessop hesitated. "Before I say more, I need your guarantee that this is all off the record. The only reason I'm sharing any information with you is because it's relevant to your safety, and measures will have to be taken to protect you."

Aiden stiffened at the implications, but he nodded. "You have my word." Safety took precedence over reporting, something Aiden had almost learned the hard way.

"Mine as well," John said.

Jessop inclined his head. "The ongoing investigation comprises international cooperation between the FBI and Interpol. We've been trying to take down an organized crime family based in London for the past eight months."

"What does that have to do with my article?" Aiden asked. He'd been digging into foreign corruption in a small European country. Not the United Kingdom.

Tapping a pen against the table, Agent Jessop met his gaze. "Organized crime is often a vast, complex beast. They usually have their fingers in everyone's pie, so to speak. The corruption is based in London but it spreads throughout several countries, including the U.S. and the country where you were investigating."

Aiden blinked in surprise. He'd assumed the people behind the corruption, and those after him, were based solely in the country where he'd uncovered the misuse of reserve funds. As they were seated deep within the government, his perception had made sense. But it looked like this whole thing was bigger than he thought.

"It's a massive operation," Agent Jessop continued. "We've been trying to pin something concrete on these people for a long time, but any witness we've uncovered has met an unfortunate end."

"Like Ingrid," Aiden muttered, before looking at the agent across the table. "I already know I'm in danger and I planned to leave town today."

Something John already knew, as Aiden had called him after walking out on his family last night.

"Yes, I'm aware," the agent said. "I've been informed of the two recent attempts on your life that have been reported to the police. I need to hear the entire story from you. Start to finish."

Aiden laid it all out for him, from the research during his time abroad, Ingrid's death, to his return to the U.S. and the ongoing threats, surveillance, and pictures. He detailed the visits he received from the stranger with the shaved head as well as the theft of his briefcase, and Agent Jessop took notes on an iPad as Aiden spoke.

"It sounds like the group has taken out a hit on you," he said, his tone grave. "It's their M.O. against anyone who speaks out or looks into them."

Aiden shivered. It was one thing to know his life was in danger, and another to hear an FBI agent say a hired killer was after him. He folded his hands together on the table, his jaw clenched.

John leaned forward in his seat. "What now?" he asked.

"Well, your article provides us with a new lead in an investigation that has been moving at a frustratingly slow pace," Jessop said. "This group is interconnected in such a way that if we can make one high-level crime stick, the whole network will come crashing down."

Aiden nodded. That was good news. Bringing down a crime organization was something any journalist would aspire to be a part of. But right now, he had more concerns than the end result of the investigation. He had his family to worry about. Brooke. Himself.

"I want to offer you both protective custody," Agent Jessop said, as if reading his mind. He glanced at John. "You might also be targeted since you are the editor who ran the article."

"What does protective custody entail?" John asked, his foot tapping consistently against the floor.

"We would start with increased security, an officer watching you at home, driving you to and from work, and depending on how the investigation goes, we might need to relocate you for your own protection."

"For how long?" John asked.

"Until we can bring charges against those who head the organization," Jessop said.

Nodding, John said, "I'd appreciate the protection."

Both men looked to Aiden, but he wasn't sure a protective detail was the right solution for him. "If it was only my life at stake, I'd say yes, but I have a big, vulnerable family. I can't risk any one of them. I need to leave as planned."

"Are you sure you want to leave your life behind when you just got home?" John asked.

"I have no choice." But this time he wouldn't be alone. He'd have Brooke with him and he wanted her protected. "Unless you think this investigation will be over soon. If you're closing in on them, my family can take extra security precautions for a limited time, but if not…"

Agent Jessop's lips thinned. "I'm afraid it might be a long time before we're ready to make any arrests. It could be years. Your instinct to go into hiding is a smart one and we can arrange that for you."

With the FBI's help, he and Brooke would be safer than if he tried to disappear on his own. "I can't leave without my fiancée. She was in the car with me the last time I was targeted. I can't risk her being here alone."

Jessop began that incessant tapping of his pen.

Aiden gritted his teeth and waited for the man's answer.

"I'll make some calls and pull some strings. Just the two of you," he said.

Aiden nodded, and let out a long sigh of relief.

None of this was good news but at least he knew the facts and the truth. False promises of wrapping up the investigation soon wouldn't do him any good.

"I have an agent waiting who will be your detail," Agent Jessop said to John. "Mr. Sterling, I'll escort you home where someone will join us later to watch the house, at least until we get your aliases and safe house set up."

Aiden's stomach churned, but he was aware this was the best possible scenario. Putting distance between himself and his family was necessary. They were way too important to be put at risk.

Agent Jessop followed him to the house in an unmarked sedan, and Aiden called Brooke along the way, telling her everything he'd learned and that he would be home soon.

He pulled up the driveway and put the car in park, the agent driving up behind him.

The front door opened, and Brooke stood in the doorway to greet him. At the sight of her, some of the heaviness weighing him down after his talk with Agent Jessop lessened. No matter what happened next, at least he had Brooke. She made all the hard stuff manageable.

He exited the vehicle and walked toward Brooke, heading around the front of the car. Movement on the side of the house caught his attention and he glanced over. A dark-haired man had stepped out from the side, as if he'd been waiting for Aiden's return, a notion that was confirmed as the man locked eyes with Aiden and raised his gun.

"Aiden!" Brooke screamed his name as she stepped out of the doorway. He ran, then dove forward, colliding with her body and taking her to the ground at the same time shots rang out.

Chapter Thirty-One

BROOKE TOOK ONE look at the man pointing a gun at Aiden and screamed. The sound of gunfire came next. Aiden slammed into her and they hit the ground hard, his body covering hers.

She lay in shock, her lungs seized up and her mind blank. She felt nothing but heart-stopping terror. She couldn't say how many shots she'd heard, but the loud bangs echoed in her ears even after things went quiet. It took a moment for clear thoughts to return, and when they did, she realized that Aiden was lying rigid on top of her.

Oh no. No, no, no.

"Aiden," she said, her voice cracking.

His face was buried in her neck, his body pressing her into the ground. She could *feel* that he was breathing, but she had no idea if he was injured. "Oh God, please be okay."

Suddenly, he moved, lifting himself up onto his elbows, his arms on either side of her head, keeping as much of her covered as possible.

At his movement, her heart began to beat again.

"Are you good?" he asked.

She released a sob. "Me? What about you? Did you... did you get hit?"

"No, sweetheart. I'm fine." He swung his gaze around and she followed his line of vision, half expecting to see the gunman standing over them with a weapon pointed at Aiden's head. But the stranger was nowhere to be seen.

"It's safe," an unfamiliar voice called out. "He's down."

"Who is that?" she asked Aiden, aware she was still shaking.

He visibly swallowed hard. "FBI." Standing, he held his hand out to her.

She grasped his palm and allowed him to pull her to her feet. Her legs shook, and he slipped an arm around her waist, holding her up. Together, they walked toward the house where a man in a suit stood over the shooter, weapon in one hand and handcuffs in the other.

The shooter lay on the ground, writhing in pain as he held on to his leg above a bleeding wound in his outer thigh.

The FBI agent kicked the man's gun far from his reach, then moved behind the shooter and cuffed his hands behind his back.

Seeing the would-be killer secured, a lightheaded feeling washed over her, and she swayed into Aiden.

He tightened his hold on her before turning them away from the scene.

"Aiden?" Alex had stepped out of the house, her mom by his side. They surveyed the scene and Lizzie gasped. Brooke broke free of Aiden, rushing over to her mother to show her she was okay before Lizzie passed out.

Everything was a blur after that. Agent Jessop called for backup and an ambulance.

Brooke's mom fussed over her, and Aiden stayed glued to her side as more FBI agents arrived to take their statements and debrief them.

Thanks to her mother's hot tea and the support of the Sterling family, who had all shown up as soon as they'd heard what happened, Brooke managed to calm down.

Hours later, Agent Jessop sat down with her and Aiden in the kitchen. The man's hair was askew, his tie undone, and he looked exhausted. She understood. *She* was emotionally drained from the entire ordeal. And something told her it wasn't over yet.

"Thank you for saving us," she blurted out, earning a brief smile from the agent before his face turned solemn again. It seemed to be his default look.

"You're welcome, Miss Snyder. Now, I want to update you all on what's going to happen next."

Aiden tensed beside her.

Jessop shook his head. "They might send someone after you again, but they'd have to move fast."

Brooke frowned. "What does that mean?"

"It means that we can directly tie this assassin to the crime family that hired him. We have his phone, a confession, and his willingness to give up names and information in return for a deal."

"He confessed?" Brooke asked, surprised. "Don't these guys usually refuse to speak, showing loyalty to *the family* and all that?"

Again, she was rewarded with a quick smile. "This isn't a mafia movie, Miss Snyder. He's not high enough up in the organization to show that kind of loyalty, but he knows enough. He'll probably get a deal for his cooperation, maybe even be put in WITSEC, but his testimony will help us take down the entire organization."

Hope and relief rushed through her, and she let out a small, choked sound. "Really?"

"Yes." Agent Jessop turned to Aiden. "You remember what I said about needing something I can pin on these people? Something serious and solid?"

Aiden nodded.

"Well, we've just found it."

Aiden let out a long exhale, his entire being deflating. Seeing relief fill him, Brooke grasped onto his hand.

"Will my family be safe?" he asked.

"It might take a few months to track down all the members of the organization, but after that, you'll be okay. Your article is going to help strengthen our case as well. Your work is going to save lives, Mr. Sterling."

At his words, pride welled up in Brooke for Aiden and the work he'd done.

With a promise to be in touch by the evening, Agent Jessop left, along with the rest of the FBI.

The family had gathered in the living room, giving Brooke and Aiden time alone.

She leaned into him, appreciating the weight of his body against hers. "I'm proud of you, Aiden."

"Thank you." With a shudder, Aiden wrapped his arms around her. Holding her tight, he brushed her temple with his lips. "God, Brooke. I've never been as scared as I was when I thought you were hurt."

She hugged him back, her chest filling with warmth. "How about we try to avoid any more drama for a while?" she suggested.

With a bark of laughter, Aiden pulled back and cupped her face, looking at her like she was precious. "I have a feeling we'll be out of touch for a while, but once the FBI says we're free, I think we should do something completely drama-free."

"Such as?" she asked, glancing up at him, filled with so much love her chest hurt.

"I was thinking about… house-hunting."

Brooke gasped. "Are you asking me to move in with you?"

"Well, I'm sure we'll be doing that in witness protection, but after that? I'm not letting you leave me."

She arched one eyebrow. "You really can't stop making decisions for me, can you?"

With another laugh, Aiden pulled her in for a kiss.

Epilogue

One Year Later

AFTER LIVING IN a small house in Idaho for eight months, Aiden and Brooke had returned to New York four months ago. While they'd been in WITSEC, Aiden had hired bodyguards in New York to protect the rest of the family, including Lizzie. It cost a fortune for the high-end security company to keep everyone safe, but it had been worth it.

The crazy in their lives came to an end when the FBI and Interpol compiled enough evidence to bring down the criminal organization behind the corruption. During the takedown, the head of the organization had been killed, as had his sons, and the rest of the group had splintered and fallen apart afterward. The arrest of many others involved came next. Those that ran were no threat to anyone.

Aiden was finally safe.

His family was, as well.

Things changed while they'd been gone, and it would take time to get reacquainted with the babies who'd grown, not to mention the family whose lives had continued in their absence. Jared returned to the office, and their dad now worked a three-day week. Alex was no longer trying to push himself too hard, but he enjoyed the stimulation the business provided. Between his father and Brooke, Jared had all the top-level support he needed.

Aiden and Brooke moved into the gatehouse. Brooke jumped back into work, eager to pick up where she'd left off at the office. Aiden, meanwhile, took on the job of house-hunting and setting up his new career, building his own online news magazine.

Turning to his laptop in the home office, he looked through the résumés sent in, excited about the future. No more traveling in favor of time with Brooke and the ability to work from home. He'd had a long eight months to create a business plan and like Brooke, he was ready to hit the ground running. Unlike Brooke, he was creating a magazine from the ground up, and building a business took time.

After about an hour at his desk, he heard the front door open and close. A moment later, the sound of Brooke's heels tapped on the floor.

"Hi, handsome," Brooke said from the doorway of the office, looking gorgeous in a flowing pale blue skirt and a cute white blouse.

"Hey, sweetheart." He closed his laptop and rose to his feet. Walking around the desk, he strode toward her and pressed a kiss to her lips.

"How was your day?" he asked.

She smiled. "Pretty good and better than your dad's." Her lips quirked upward in a grin.

He raised his eyebrows. "Oh? What happened?"

"Someone brought donuts into the break room this morning. He thought he could get away with just one." She shook her head at his father's antics.

"And you caught him?" Aiden guessed.

She nodded. "The poor man begged me not to tell and to let him have just one."

"Let me guess. You were strict and mean."

"Be nice!" Brooke playfully slapped his shoulder. "Someone has to make sure he's staying healthy when my mom isn't around. But we negotiated. He said half. I let him have half of his half." She met his gaze. "And I never promised not to tell my mother."

Aiden burst out laughing. His poor dad. Someone watched every move he made.

Brooke told him about the rest of her day, chatting animatedly about the job Jared had put her on with a long-time VP. She really loved her work, and while Aiden couldn't understand why, he was glad. Her eyes lit up as she talked, and a feeling of peace and happiness settled over him. He was so damned grateful she had given him a second chance.

Their time away merely cemented the bond they'd

been rebuilding. Brooke was everything to him, and after five long years away, he finally had the life he wanted.

He thought about the ring box in the top drawer of his desk. He'd spent hours with a jeweler picking out the perfect stone and design, then decided to wait until they walked into their new house for the first time.

Looking at Brooke now, he wondered why he was waiting. He didn't want to wait another moment to see his ring on her finger. And despite the progress they'd made as a couple, he needed to hear her say she'd be his in every way.

He knew Brooke didn't want a big production or proposal. She wasn't the type to want something flashy or impressive. She just needed him the same way he needed her.

Taking her hand, Aiden led her around his desk and pulled open the drawer.

She looked inside and at the sight of the little black velvet box, her eyes went wide. "Aiden?"

He pulled it out, ready to give the speech of a lifetime.

Dropping to one knee, he took her hand in his. "Brooke, you have been in my life for so long, I now can't imagine what it's like without you. Hell, I was dumb enough to try, and I never want to go through that torture again."

Her damp eyes met his and her hand shook, but she waited patiently, listening to every word he had to say. And he had plenty.

He smiled. "I want to wake up beside you every day and go to bed holding you each night. I want to start a family together and enjoy all the big and small things life brings. I want it all, but mostly, I want you in every way."

He flipped open the box. "Brooklyn Snyder, will you forgive me for every mistake I ever made and trust I will do my very best to never hurt you again? Will you marry me?"

Brooke blinked and tears rolled down her cheeks, but her smile was wide as she nodded. "Yes, Aiden. Yes to everything. To a life together, to a family, to forgiveness always, and to forever."

He pulled out the emerald-cut four-carat diamond set in a platinum diamond band—because Brooke deserved nothing less—and slid it onto her hand.

"This is too much!" she said, but she was crying and still smiling at the same time.

"Nothing is too much for you." Aiden hugged her, lifting her off her feet and kissing her for a good long while. When he finally released her, he asked, "Want to go next door and tell the parents?"

Though he'd love to end this proposal in bed, he

knew his soon-to-be wife too well. She'd want to share the news with her mom. And he wanted to spread the good news to his father and tell his dad that Brooke would officially be part of their family. He also had a hunch Alex would be popping the question to Lizzie very soon.

Once the parents knew, the sibling phone chain would begin.

If that meant Aiden had to wait to get Brooke into bed later tonight? That was just fine. They were beginning the rest of their lives together, and he couldn't wait.

Thanks for reading! Next up: The final book in the Sterling Family series.

Read JUST ONE MORE DATE

A fake dating, holiday romance novella.

JUST ONE MORE DATE

Leo Watson needs a pretend wife for a business Christmas party.

Could the cute barista who serves his favorite coffee drink play the part?

Camille Hendricks is willing… *for a price*—an interview at his sister's PR company.

The game seems easy but their attraction is all too real.

When sexy lines are crossed, both Leo and Cammie stand to lose something more important than business.

They risk losing each other.

Read JUST ONE MORE DATE

Want even more Carly books?

CARLY'S BOOKLIST by Series – visit:
https://www.carlyphillips.com/CPBooklist

Sign up for Carly's Newsletter:
https://www.carlyphillips.com/CPNewsletter

Join Carly's Corner on Facebook:
https://www.carlyphillips.com/CarlysCorner

Carly on Facebook:
https://www.carlyphillips.com/CPFanpage

Carly on Instagram:
https://www.carlyphillips.com/CPInstagram

Carly's Booklist

The Kingstons — newest series first

The Sterling Family
Book 1: Just One More Moment (Remington Sterling & Raven Walsh)
Book 2: Just One More Dare (Dex Kingston & Samantha Dare)
Book 3: Just One More Mistletoe (Max Corbin & Brandy Bloom)
Book 4: Just One More Temptation (Noah Powers & Fallon Sterling)
Book 5: Just One More Affair (Charlotte Kendall & Jared Sterling)
Book 6: Just One More Time (Brooke Snyder & Aiden Sterling)
Novella: Just One More Date (Leo Watson & Camille Hendricks)

The Kingston Family
Book 1: Just One Night (Linc Kingston & Jordan Greene)
Book 2: Just One Scandal (Chloe Kingston & Beck Daniels)
Book 3: Just One Chance (Xander Kingston & Sasha Keaton)
Book 4: Just One Spark (Dash Kingston & Cassidy Forrester)

Novella: Just Another Spark (Dash Kingston & Cassidy Forrester)
Book 5: Just One Wish (Axel Forrester)
Book 6: Just One Dare (Aurora Kingston & Nick Dare)
Book 7: Just One Kiss (Knox Sinclair & Jade Dare)
Book 8: Just One Taste (Asher Dare & Nicolette Bettencourt)
Book 9: Just One Fling (Harrison Dare & Winter Capwell)
Book 10: Just One Tease (Zach Dare & Hadley Stevens)
Book 10.5: Just One Summer (Maddox James & Gabriella Davenport)

The Dares — newest series first

Dare Nation
Book 1: Dare to Resist (Austin & Quinn)
Book 2: Dare to Tempt (Damon & Evie)
Book 3: Dare to Play (Jaxon & Macy)
Book 4: Dare to Stay (Brandon & Willow)
Novella: Dare to Tease (Hudson & Brianne)

* Paul Dare's sperm donor kids

The Sexy Series
Book 1: More Than Sexy (Jason Dare & Faith)
Book 2: Twice As Sexy (Tanner & Scarlett)
Book 3: Better Than Sexy (Landon & Vivienne)
Novella: Sexy Love (Shane & Amber)

The Knight Brothers
Book 1: Take Me Again (Sebastian & Ashley)
Book 2: Take Me Down (Parker & Emily)
Book 3: Dare Me Tonight (Ethan Knight & Sienna Dare)
Novella: Take The Bride (Sierra & Ryder)
Take Me Now – Short Story (Harper & Matt)

NY Dares Series (NY Dare Cousins)
Book 1: Dare to Surrender (Gabe & Isabelle)
Book 2: Dare to Submit (Decklan & Amanda)
Book 3: Dare to Seduce (Max & Lucy)

Dare to Love Series
Book 1: Dare to Love (Ian & Riley)
Book 2: Dare to Desire (Alex & Madison)
Book 3: Dare to Touch (Dylan & Olivia)
Book 4: Dare to Hold (Scott & Meg)
Book 5: Dare to Rock (Avery & Grey)
Book 6: Dare to Take (Tyler & Ella)
A Very Dare Christmas – Short Story (Ian & Riley)

** Sienna Dare gets together with Ethan Knight in **The Knight Brothers** (Dare Me Tonight).*

** Jason Dare gets together with Faith in the **Sexy Series** (More Than Sexy).*

For the most recent Carly books, visit CARLY'S BOOKLIST page
www.carlyphillips.com/CPBooklist

Other Indie Series — newest series first

Hot Heroes Series
Book 1: Touch You Now (Kane & Halley)
Book 2: Hold You Now (Jake & Phoebe)
Book 3: Need You Now (Braden & Juliette)
Book 4: Want You Now (Kyle & Andi)

Bodyguard Bad Boys
Book 1: Rock Me (Ben & Summer)
Book 2: Tempt Me (Austin & Mia)
Novella: His To Protect (Shane & Talia)

Billionaire Bad Boys
Book 1: Going Down Easy (Kaden & Lexie)
Book 2: Going Down Fast (Lucas & Maxie)
Book 3: Going Down Hard (Derek & Cassie)
Book 4: Going In Deep (Julian & Kendall)
Going Down Again – Short Story (Kaden & Lexie)

For the most recent Carly books, visit CARLY'S BOOKLIST page
www.carlyphillips.com/CPBooklist

Carly's Originally Traditionally Published Books

Serendipity's Finest Series
Book 1: Perfect Fit (Mike & Cara)
Book 2: Perfect Fling (Cole & Erin)
Book 3: Perfect Together (Sam & Nicole)
Book 4: Perfect Strangers (Luke & Alexa)

Serendipity Series
Book 1: Serendipity (Ethan & Faith)
Book 2: Kismet (Trevor & Lissa)
Book 3: Destiny (Nash & Kelly)
Book 4: Fated (Nick & Kate)
Book 5: Karma (Dare & Liza)

Costas Sisters
Book 1: Under the Boardwalk (Quinn & Ariana)
Book 2: Summer of Love (Ryan & Zoe)

Ty and Hunter
Book 1: Cross My Heart (Ty & Lilly)
Book 2: Sealed with a Kiss (Hunter & Molly)

The Lucky Series
Book 1: Lucky Charm (Derek & Gabrielle)
Book 2: Lucky Streak (Mike & Amber)
Book 3: Lucky Break (Jason & Lauren)

The Most Eligible Bachelor Series
Book 1: Kiss Me if You Can (Sam & Lexie)
Book 2: Love Me If You Dare (Rafe & Sara)

The Hot Zone
Book 1: Hot Stuff (Brandon & Annabelle)
Book 2: Hot Number (Damian & Micki)
Book 3: Hot Item (Riley & Sophie)
Book 4: Hot Property (John & Amy)

The Chandler Brothers
Book 1: The Bachelor (Roman & Charlotte)
Book 2: The Playboy (Rick & Kendall)
Book 3: The Heartbreaker (Chase & Sloane)

The Simply Series
Book 1: Simply Sinful (Kane & Kayla)
Book 2: Simply Scandalous (Logan & Catherine)
Book 3: Simply Sensual (Ben & Gracie)
Book 4: Body Heat (Jake & Brianne)
Book 5: Simply Sexy (Colin & Rina)

Carly Classics
Book 1: The Right Choice (Mike & Carly)
Book 2: Perfect Partners (Griffin & Chelsie)
Book 3: Unexpected Chances (Dylan & Holly)
Book 4: Worthy of Love (Kevin & Nikki)

For the most recent Carly books, visit CARLY'S BOOKLIST page
www.carlyphillips.com/CPBooklist

Carly's Still Traditionally Published Books

Stand-Alone Books
Brazen
Secret Fantasy
Seduce Me
The Seduction
More Than Words Volume 7 – Compassion Can't Wait
Naughty Under the Mistletoe
Grey's Anatomy 101 Essay

For the most recent Carly books, visit CARLY'S BOOKLIST page
www.carlyphillips.com/CPBooklist

About the Author

NY Times, Wall Street Journal, and USA Today Bestseller, Carly Phillips is the queen of Alpha Heroes, at least according to The Harlequin Junkie Reviewer. Carly married her college sweetheart and lives in Purchase, NY along with her crazy dogs who are featured on her Facebook and Instagram pages. The author of over 75 romance novels, she has raised two incredible daughters and is now an empty nester. Carly's book, The Bachelor, was chosen by Kelly Ripa as her first romance club pick. Carly loves social media and interacting with her readers. Want to keep up with Carly? Sign up for her newsletter and receive TWO FREE books at www.carlyphillips.com.

Made in the USA
Middletown, DE
06 September 2025